MW01088247

"The great thing is to last . . . and write when there is something that you know . . ."

Ernest Hemingway

"I am ready to be the first to humiliate myself. Hence, the pothouse! Honoured sir, a month ago Mr. Lebeziatnikov gave my wife a beating, and my wife is a very different matter from me. Do you understand? Allow me to ask you another question out of simple curiosity: have you ever spent a night on a hay barge, on the Neva?"

Fyodor Dostoevsky

"And as for you of the brown acid and lyrical flights of fancy, I do sometimes find it curious that you've selected this hobby of writing as opposed to say, tennis or car restoration. Every instinct you have pulls against the rules. You are the dancer with one leg. Fortunately, I've read enough of your prose to know that one-legged dancers sometimes perform the most curious little pirouettes."

Personal letter from Smibst (01/08)

OTHER BOOKS BY THIS AUTHOR

Gooks In The Wire

Eskimo Gibberish

Electric—Return Of The Ironist

Zipperhead

Plate Of Shrimp

Year Of Famine

Oose Termini

One Thing You Can't Hide

Doctor of Pipes

STRANGE AND LOVING COMMUNIQUES FROM INSIDE THE BRIAR BROTHERHOOD

Ralph William Larsen

DOCTOR OF PIPES
STRANGE AND LOVING COMMUNIQUES FROM
INSIDE THE BRIAR BROTHERHOOD

Copyright © 2013, 2015 Ralph William Larsen.

All rights reserved. No part of this book may be used or reproduced by any means, graphic, electronic, or mechanical, including photocopying, recording, taping or by any information storage retrieval system without the written permission of the publisher except in the case of brief quotations embodied in critical articles and reviews.

This is a work of fiction. All of the characters, names, incidents, organizations, and dialogue in this novel are either the products of the author's imagination or are used fictitiously.

iUniverse books may be ordered through booksellers or by contacting:

iUniverse
1663 Liberty Drive
Bloomington, IN 47403
www.iuniverse.com
1-800-Authors (1-800-288-4677)

Because of the dynamic nature of the Internet, any web addresses or links contained in this book may have changed since publication and may no longer be valid. The views expressed in this work are solely those of the author and do not necessarily reflect the views of the publisher, and the publisher hereby disclaims any responsibility for them.

Any people depicted in stock imagery provided by Thinkstock are models, and such images are being used for illustrative purposes only. Certain stock imagery © Thinkstock.

ISBN: 978-1-4917-0176-8 (sc)
ISBN: 978-1-4917-0177-5 (e)

Printed in the United States of America.

iUniverse rev. date: 01/28/2015

Dedication

In fond memory of Bill Unger, secretary/treasurer of the North American Society of Pipe Collectors, editor of the Pipe Collector Newsletter, tireless champion of the Briar Brotherhood and, mercifully, the first human to dare publish a single word of my written shenanigans. Thanks for all of that, Bill.

FRONT AND REAR COVER DESIGN AND ALL
INTERIOR ILLUSTRATIONS—
"MR. LIZARD"—MICHAEL JODRY

BACK COVER PHOTOGRAPH
AND WHATEVER WORD EDITING
GOT DONE
(if you spot a typo or two or three
it's not her fault, it's mine)
"TEA KID"—DIANE KHOURY

FRONT COVER PHOTOGRAPH
YOLANDA SAAYMAN
"LEGENDE"
YOLANDA SAAYMAN PHOTOGRAPHY
CAPE TOWN, SOUTH AFRICA
COPYRIGHT YOLANDA SAAYMAN

"THANKS, GUYS!"

Introduction—
The Great American
Pipe Smoking Essay

If memory serves me well—and if truth be known, of late memory hasn't been serving me at all—somebody sometime may have said something along the lines of "if your expectations have an annoying habit of outrunning your talent, the smart move might be to hobble your expectations." Norman Mailer and Ernest Hemingway, a celebrated brace of American egoists if ever there was one, both boasted publicly of intending to write the Great American Novel. My aspirations in picking up the proverbial pen here were far less grandiose. My modest aim was simply to have some fun. And okay, yes, I admit it. The thought did cross my mind that I might just be able to capture one of literature's less prestigious flags. Something analogous, I suppose, to taking home an Oscar for best animated short documentary in a language nobody speaks or understands. I connived to do nothing more—and nothing less, mind you—than attempt to write the Great American Pipe Smoking Essay.

After a year or so in harness to that ambition, it pleases me now to think of all the words that have followed as one might a two-legged circus chair. The one leg, as I see it, is an abiding faith that pipemen are, as a general rule, deep thinkers. I've heard tell that most can, and some actually do, smoke and think at the same time. The second leg of my rickety teeter chair is an equally abiding suspicion that hardcore pipe puffers are a resilient lot. It's as if they've been inoculated in some mysterious way by their tobacco addictive natures against those ailments brought on by the occasional strange read. Anyway, that's my theory, and within the pages of this modest little book, I'm sticking by it.

For, you see, I have this genuine affection for all pipe smokers. Earned or unearned, I give them credit for having minds that are receptive to the unusual. I think they "get it." They recognize and appreciate when a guy is just having a little fun in print . . . sometimes maybe even at their expense. Yeah, when I think of pipe smokers, especially pipe smokers who read pipe journals in lieu of Field and Stream or TV Guide, I enjoy believing maybe, just maybe, I've found a potential receptive audience for some of my off-the-wall pseudo-journalism.

And if I'm mistaken, so what? At least with pipe smokers you can make an error like that and not get your jaw broken. 'Cause pipe smokers are nowhere near as dangerous as their demonic first cousins, the stogie chewers. I suspect most of those grunting pug-noses haven't an inkling that Cigar Aficionado is a magazine, and couldn't read it even if they did. The brown-juice-spitting Neanderthals who chew the pointy ends of White Owls and Dutch Masters into gummy blobs tend to think with their fists. They'll punch you in the kisser just for putting them on!

So yes, I've taken careful measure of my more gentrified briar-obsessed readership here, and cunningly calculated that I can get away with taking some journalistic liberties. For instance, I don't believe I've written a single piece that is exclusively about briar. Because, you see, the discussion of pipes and tobacco is for me usually just a safe harbor from which to set sail for some faraway greater understanding. So when I'm working well, yes, there will be the pipes and the tobacco. But then, hopefully, there will be more.

And I don't hold it against myself, and I'm hoping you won't either, if the things I've lasted long enough to know and am now attempting to write about are not exactly run-of-the-mill stuff. If attending my first pipe show made me feel like a sexual deviant, I'm gonna cop to it. And if the only pre-transition Barling pipe I can afford has two large cracks in the bowl that leak smoke like it had ears on fire, well, you're gonna hear about that travesty too.

I've taken off the literary gloves here, people. I've done it partially, I suppose, because somewhere in my writerly (no such word, don't bother looking it up) DNA a bully lurks. But then there is this as well: I've done it because I believe you guys, the resilient pipemen of this world, my mildly nicotine-addicted heroes, can take every silly word I dish out and do it smoking.

Table of Nonsense

Doctor of Pipes

STRANGE AND LOVING COMMUNIQUES
FROM INSIDE THE BRIAR BROTHERHOOD

Table of Nonsense Redux

Original Michael Jodry Artwork

Doctor of Pipes

Rumpled bed sheets. The work clothing stacked in your hands is chin high as you move silently toward the early morning doorway and the stairs and the coffeepot and the hundred monstrous daytime things waiting to confront you. But something gives you pause. Your wife is lying there, still asleep. Maybe she has pajamas on. Maybe she doesn't. You stand there looking down, and as surely as you know anything, you know you are standing at the center of your world, true north on the compass of your life. And like all those unseen cosmic magnets tugging at all those quivering little campers' needles, you too feel a pull. It is the urge to remain, to resist the hubbub of the work-a-day world and climb back into bed. But then there is that counter-pull, the need to earn a paycheck for children who like to eat. So maybe you don't. Or maybe you do. But either way, the pull to stay is tangible.

I mention all this because last Sunday I set my alarm and got up with the sun to go downstairs to turn on the Turkish Grand Prix. I do this during the racing season, get up early on the only day I can sleep late to watch little open-wheeled racing cars chasing each other around my television screen. The expectation is that all such mornings born of repetitiveness rather than enthusiasm will be about the same. But last Sunday something was slightly askew. My pipes—well, some of my pipes anyway—sit in a three-tiered Decatur rack to the right of my living room window. On the best of days, through these panes streams Mr. Sun, his smiling morning face surgically striated by a set of partially opened venetian blinds. Long

1

alternating lines of light and dark fall across my pipes and their mahogany rack. The pipes themselves, all seasoned veterans smoked to hues ranging from honey brown to dark amber, positively glow in that staggered shimmer. On such a stage they transcend their nighttime roles as utilitarian objects arrayed upon a table. They become for me a work of art, a bouquet of complementary colors that skins my eyes and delights my senses.

And last Sunday, standing transfixed above my pipes, caught up in their little show, I made a small confession to myself. The feeling I was experiencing felt alarmingly akin to that old familiar pull I've so often experienced poised above my sleeping wife. "No shame in that," you say. "Nothing being said here that doesn't strike a responsive chord with damn near every red-blooded pipeman in the world." And I agree . . . to a degree. I mean, so long as the object being gazed down upon with lust in the heart is a partially clad woman in sleepy repose, no alarm need sound. But what do you say about someone, or more personally, someone who happens to be yourself, who feels a very similar physical attraction toward oily old objects crafted from the bulbous roots of Mediterranean shrubs?

I know. To some this may seem a bit far-fetched. But the shock of that realization set me to thinking. How many pleasant moments, moments over a near lifetime that in their totality might now conceivably amount to months if not years, have I spent fondling one pipe or another in my hand, rolling it lovingly between adoring fingers, allowing my eyes to possess it in ways best described in words culled from the lexicon of love? And not platonic love. Oh no, not platonic by a longshot. The just-so feminine curve of a particular shank and stem, the warm, snug fit of a shapely bowl in the inwardly curled knot of a sweaty palm, the curious way closely watched tobacco smoke seems to cling to the polished round of a pipe rim before reluctantly deciding it simply must let go and be up and away.

These are sensuous observations, matters of the groin moved upward into the hands and eyes.

Feel free to scoff at my words if they trouble you in any way. But let's face it. Deep down in the secret Laundromat where all the real mental wash gets done, we are, every last pipe puffing son-of-a-gun of us, masters of self-deception. So next time you find yourself in that ultra-private little pipe smoking place of yours, doing all the naughty things I've just described, know this. ralph in jersey, doctor of pipes in ways having nothing whatsoever to do with patent numbers and fishtailed stampings, has your unique condition diagnosed. As a fellow sufferer, he has fearlessly sounded the depth of our shared wood-borne depravity. He, for one, is as far out of the closet as any pipe puffer can possibly get with his clothes still on.

Sense of It All

God forgive me, but when Auntie June called to say Uncle Ern had passed, all I could think about was his favorite pipe, a Barling lumberman with the cherished oval BARLING MAKE and YE OLDE WOOD stamped along its long, dark, oily shank. So after making perfunctory inquiries about the details of my uncle's death and Auntie June's state of well-being, I thoroughly disgraced myself by getting right down to brass tacks.

"Say, Auntie June, I know you've got a lot on your plate at the moment what with the funeral and all, but as a pipe smoker I just have to ask. Have you given any thought as to what's to become of Uncle Ern's pipes? Especially that long one he always seemed to have sticking out of his mouth?"

Not surprisingly, my monstrously mistimed and utterly inappropriate question seemed to wound my aunt as a gunshot might. After an uncomfortable pause filled with nothing but malignant silence, my aunt picked up our conversation on a noticeably cooler note.

"As the other pipe smoker in the family, you should know better than anyone how much those silly pipes meant to your uncle. I swear, I think he loved that long thin one more than he loved me. I can tell you, he never tried smoking me in the shower or carrying me around in his shirt pocket behind that stupid noisy lawnmower. So when that strange old man Edgar Gower down at Maudlin's Funeral Home suggested we cremate Uncle Ern right along with his favorite pipe, well, it just seemed the right thing to do."

What could I say? The plan my aunt had put in place seemed so irrevocable. It was, I supposed, now simply my turn to get acquainted with pain akin to being gunshot. From my end of the line there came not an audible word, although I suppose my long loud exhale of indignant disgust must have burst through my aunt's phone loud and clear as a vile epithet.

"God knows, thinking back now there must be a hundred or more times I've seen and heard you licking your lips and telling your Uncle Ern just how much you coveted his little pipe. Why, I remember one particularly uncomfortable evening of repeated beggings that ended with your uncle half-joking to me in the car on the way home that 'if I should ever come to a violent end, June, just tell the police it was my nephew for sure who killed me for my pipe.' So yes, I do know how much that pipe meant to you. But what's done is done. I've just come from Maudlin's. I've said my final goodbye to my beloved Ernest."

A catch in her voice was followed by a telltale gulp and a single unguarded sniffle.

"For all the good stupid smoking pipes do anyone in the Hereafter, Uncle Ern's beloved Barling is sticking out of the breast pocket of his blue blazer, pressed for eternity against his heart. I placed it there myself not an hour ago. Now the two of them will be together for eternity . . . or at least till they get to the crematorium"

With this my aunt positively cackled. Unnerving for sure. But I chalked it up to an unhealthy cocktail of intense grief and maybe a few too many of those triangular little pills the women of my family swallow like candy at family funerals.

"It's done," Auntie June finished. "Mr. Gower has closed and sealed the coffin. Everything is done."

This last proclamation was said with such finality that it didn't even seem rude when Auntie June just hung up. I could actually hear it happening. As our uncomfortable little chat had wobbled along, my aunt's voice had audibly turned inward. It was exactly as though her parting remark, "Everything is done," had been addressed purely to herself, not me. Then, having said all there was to say to herself, having heard all she needed to hear, she'd done what anyone taking handfuls of triangular pills would. She'd forgotten someone else was on the line, placed the phone back in its cradle and gone to lie down.

In less than a half-hour I was at Maudlin's Funeral Home. I won't call its director, Edgar Gower, a friend. Men as strange as Edgar Gower don't have friends. They have family that can't disavow them and they have acquaintances. Edgar and I are acquaintances. I suppose we've been aware of each other's existence since high school. And the second Wednesday of every other month we meet at Skiddles Chophouse for dinner and a smoke. Not, like I say, because we are friends. It just happens we belong to the same pipe smoker's club. And that right there is a condition I've been meaning to correct. I wish I could tell you that Edgar Gower was the only odd duck at those meetings, but he isn't. Sometimes it seems half the people I meet who smoke pipes and every person I know who belongs to a pipe smoker's club are just plain too weird for words. Why I go to those meetings every second month like clockwork, and for that matter why I look forward to each and every one of them as if it was my birthday, is a mystery to me. I can tell you that!

But that's neither here nor there. All you need to know is now I'm sticking my head in the door of Edgar Gower's creepy little office and saying, "Edgar, I've just gotten off the phone with my Auntie June and I've come to pay final respects to Uncle Ern. I know visiting hours are not for another couple hours, but this is the only time I was gonna have to get by. Mind if I have a few moments alone to say my good-byes?"

What's the guy gonna say, "no"? Edgar Gower is a funeral director. His job, his life's mission is to sooth and accommodate. The doctors' motto is "First do no harm." With funeral directors it's "First cause no consternation." I'd counted on that.

So now I'm standing in this too cold room. It's just me in there with the half-light and maybe three dozen empty folding chairs and the sealed coffin of Uncle Ern. Ever wonder how a coffin gets "sealed" and what you'd have to do to unseal one if you really had to? Well, I can tell you the answer is not much. Futzing with the long thin pick on my trusty Czechoslovakian three-way pipe tool, it took me all of about thirty seconds to undo the lid on Uncle Ern's box. 'Cause my plan from the beginning was to substitute the Barling lumberman in Uncle Ern's blazer pocket with a ringer pipe I'd brought along for that specific purpose.

Now I'm not one for blowing my own horn, but I will tell you this. A man with no conscience would've driven down to Maudlin's and taken Ern's pipe and not given a hoot. I mean, the whole idea of dead people needing or wanting or caring about smoking pipes is a complete crock, right? But not only had I gone to the bother of digging Ern up a substitute briar, I'd even picked him out a piece a dead man wouldn't necessarily be ashamed to be seen with—ignoring for the moment the unlikelihood of cremated dead men being seen with anything. Okay, sure, the GBD lumberman I'd brought along was no pre-transition Barling and on its best day had always been a below average smoker. But the way I figured it, Uncle Ern was in no condition to notice.

Only trouble was, when I opened the lid there was Uncle Ern and his blue blazer as expected. But the breast pocket where Auntie June had told me she'd personally put my uncle's pipe was empty. But it wasn't gone! Shockingly, inexplicably, somehow, within a sealed box that by all reason should have contained no living thing capable of movement, somehow the Barling lumberman had been mysteriously transported into my uncle's hand. There was no missing it. In its pallid setting of powdered dead skin, the gemlike blackness of the pipe's match-scorched rim jumped up at the eye like a bug on a white bed sheet. And my uncle's cold dead hand wasn't simply holding the pipe. Oh no. It was being positively cradled in that loving way only a seasoned pipe smoker comes to master, the bowl of it buried snuggly in the deep recess created by palm and inward curling fingers.

It was the hint of a smile at the corners of my uncle's fixed lips that finally stopped me in my tracks. This is a bit difficult to explain, but it was as though in lifting that lid I'd interrupted a very private and not entirely unhappy shared moment between a dead man and his favorite pipe. To intrude further seemed unthinkable. As an act of contrition, I closed the lid as softly and reverently as my shaking hands would allow, all thoughts of stealing from the dead thoroughly expunged from my brain. And so, two days later, as per Auntie June's wishes, Uncle Ern and this pre-transition Barling lumberman faced the fires of cremation, and perhaps eternity as well, together.

A few months would go by before I'd face Edgar Gower over drinks at Skiddles Chophouse. In that time I did a lot of thinking about what happens to people after they die. Never the most religious of men, you might even say I'd begun to come around. Way I figured it, if a dead man could remove a pipe from his pocket and place it in his hand, then all bets were off and anything was possible.

That evening at Skiddles Edgar Gower confessed under the liberating influence of several Glenlivets that it was his handwork I'd discovered. After Auntie June had left the funeral home, as an odd fellow in that odd fraternity calling itself the Brotherhood of the Briar, Edgar had gotten it into his odd head how cruel it might have seemed to him to be left lying there dead in his coffin, the best damn pipe in the world right there in his breast pocket and him not being able to get at it. So as a man practiced in the ways of both pipe and cadaver manipulation, Edgar had taken it upon himself to place that pre-transition Barling lumberman inside the curl of my Uncle Ern's stiff dead fingers. A man not immune to professional hubris, a pale and red-eyed Edgar Gower insisted I understand that "with rigor mortis having entered the equation, it had been an operation requiring both the utmost skill and delicacy."

And that wasn't the all of it. Edgar further confessed he'd even contemplated placing the Barling between my uncle's lips. But then he'd confronted the logistical difficulties of closing the lid, the lumberman being long, the space between my uncle's face and the linen liner of the coffin short. And this crazy thought had come to him as well. Was not having the world's greatest pipe stuck between your lips for eternity with no hope of ever getting any tobacco or a match and even if you did, having dead hands that would not serve you, simply an act of compound cruelty? So that strange evening, thinking himself a compassionate pipeman, Edgar Gower had done all he'd felt advisable and not one iota more. For my part, out amongst the dead on a zombie-like stroll of greed and possession, I'd stumbled upon Edgar's handwork. Understandably, I think, I'd misunderstood all I was witnessing and for a short time it altered me spiritually.

Now, over a few calming drinks and several bowls of strong tobacco, Edgar and I, acquaintances since high school, attempted in words that seemed not quite up to the task to get all we'd done off our chests. As fellow members of the same strange pipe smoker's club, we sat there puffing away and attempting to make sense of it all.

Pipemen Out
of Control

Did you ever get a pipe in the mail you really, really didn't want? I got one like that last week. It's a GBD bent rhodesian, shape #9438. Fifty years ago, when I first saw this particular pipe, it was nestled in its little felt pipe sock within a bright yellow box. Its Century finish was the warm gold of afternoon sunshine passing through aged cognac in fine crystal. Now, heavily caked, it's been rubbed down with savage, repeated usage to the flat brown of a mature hickory shell. It is, in short, everything I cherish in a used pipe, and because of the note that's come with it, I'd give 'most anything to have never received it.

In the late 1960s, Danny "Little Red" Hollingsworth and I were a couple of out-of-control kids who just happened to love pipes. Somehow, some way, we found each other, and then, in a major miscarriage of sound business practice, became co-managers of an upscale tobacco shop. To the untrained customer eye we must have seemed a couple of polite clerks, semi-knowledgeable mixers of tobacco in large wooden bowls and enthusiastic pitchmen for expensive briars and cigars. But when the door swung shut behind those customers and we were left alone with all those high-end pipes, real lunacy took hold. Like a couple of Christmas morning kids, we'd tear through those multi-colored pipe boxes and velvet pipe socks, ogling and tossing about one highly polished smoking treasure after another. Alcoholics in a distillery, sex addicts in a whorehouse, Egyptologists run amuck in King Tut's tomb, Red and I were pipemen out of control.

Then came the night we were summoned to "the warehouse." As luck would have it, our shop was owned by a major importer of English pipes into the United States. And unlike all days before in which we would order a small quantity of pipes for our in-house inventory and wait for them to arrive several days later at the hands of Mustache Chuck the smiling UPS delivery guy, this evening we were being invited to go up to the mothership and pick out our pipes.

Now picture this, "The warehouse" was the size of a small aircraft hangar, but the only "planes" in it were pipes and pipe boxes stacked row upon row on metal shelving stretching floor-to-ceiling for about as far as the eye could see. There were more Comoy pipes in that one cavernous room than could be ogled in a month of Sundays. There were GBD pipes of every line and description, Virgins in their little red boxes, Centuries in their yellow, Sablees in brown, a wall-high rainbow of multi-colored pipe boxes and pipe socks and shiny, waiting-to-be-smoked pipes. Why, most pipe collectors consider themselves fortunate if they've seen a single GBD Unique nestled in its imperial blue, velvet-lined box. That crazy, out-of-control night Red and I saw a hundred. And it was all too, too much for us. We simply ran amuck.

Like all other human activities that are too pleasurable for the mind to take in all at once, in retrospect our time inside the warehouse went by in a blur. I do remember losing track of Red in all that euphoric chaos. I have this vague recollection of sitting spread-eagled on a cold concrete floor, drunk to physical collapse with pipe lust, surrounded not by empty whiskey pints but rather by dozens of opened and pushed aside pipe boxes. I think I recall hearing Red one or two rows away, lost in his own reverie, chanting to himself over and over again, "Man, just look at this. Look at this. Look at this."

Next thing I remember is being outside, half running, half stumbling across a dark parking lot. Then Red and I are sitting in our car, and by its totally inadequate dashboard lights we're literally howling with delight. I think now of how lucky we were that it was winter in New Jersey and the windows were rolled up so no responsible adult within earshot could overhear our shenanigans. We pulled one pipe after another from two bulging shopping bags, each of us insanely intent on sharing our discovered treasures with the other. Red and I were two young adults the night of our epic encounter with "the warehouse." We should have been able to get a handle on our emotions. But we weren't. Because like a couple of four-year-olds, we'd just discovered what it felt like to be set loose in Santa's workshop with an open line of credit.

The pipe that has come in the mail is one of the first pipes Red pulled from his bag that evening. For sure there were more expensive and impressive pieces I might have coveted from his harvest, but I've always been into small, classically-shaped English pipes. To me, a GBD bent rhodesian, model #9438 is about as good as it gets. And that baby of Red's had birdseye that would make a peacock green with envy. It was a birdseye pipe like no other birdseye pipe. Because as improbable as this sounds, Red's #9438 had no cross-grain anywhere, just 360 degrees of the world's most gorgeous briar dots and rings radiating from a single point at the very bottom of the bowl and going everywhere. Man oh man, did I want that pipe.

I recall thinking my best hope of getting it was a pipe in my bag I had absolutely no recollection of having come across or selected. But there it was within a black leather bag within a hinged green case, a little full-bent W.O. Larsen freehand in the shape of a crescent moon, perfect form-bent straight grain running up each of its dark-stained flanks, its face a dimpled masterpiece etched from the most eye-catching plateau grain either of us had ever seen. And Red loved freehands. Red loved this W.O. the way I loved his GBD rhodesian. A deal seemed possible. But strangely, neither of us seemed capable of giving up what we already had. Maybe it was all the free-flowing adrenaline of the moment that sped up time, but somehow that bond of affection any pipe smoker expects will gradually grow between himself and his pipes seemed almost instantaneous on that strange night. So no pipes exchanged hands between Red and me that night or any other night over the last fifty years.

It seemed the best bargain we could strike was a verbal pact. If and when either of us passed away, we each promised to arrange to get our special pipe to the other. And last week, accompanied by a one-line note in the unmistakably neat and flowery hand of a woman, Red's bent rhodesian arrived at my door. The note says simply "Ralph. Red wanted you to have this one. I am so very, very sorry. Christine."

I've had a week now to think about my old buddy Red and what exactly to do with this most unwanted but dearly beloved little pipe. My wonderful wife, god bless her little, selfish heart, has taken to screaming at the top of her surprisingly powerful lungs, "You carry that damn pipe around this house the way the dog does his bone. So help me, if I see you moon-eyeing that worthless piece of junk one more time, I'll break it in two myself and throw the pieces in the trash." So time is not on my side here.

For its own protection I've had to put Red's pipe under lock and key. Today, when the old battle-ax was out garage saleing, I pulled down the W.O. freehand that Red always coveted. From within its green, hinged box, I removed the note I'd penned just in case I'd gone first. Of the hundred or so pipes I presently possess, the W.O. is the only one I've never smoked. By the childish rule of "finders keepers" it was mine, but somehow, by some higher rule I'd chosen to ignore, in my heart I've always known it was Red's. But Red was gone now, so I figured it was time. So I packed it full of my favorite blend, crazily overpriced Compton's Macedonian Mixture, and fired that baby up. Memories of my old friend Red came flooding over me as I assumed they might . . . but they weren't the ones I might have expected.

Maybe that beautiful pipe had something to do with it. Surprisingly, it smoked like a total rat. No match seemed capable of keeping it lit for long, and for whatever brief interlude it did allow me to puff on it, it radiated heat into my poor, suffering hand as if it were a super-heated charcoal briquette caught up in the fury of a blacksmith's bellows. So as I cursed that W.O., I remembered how Red and I had stayed in touch by phone and e-mail this last half-century, but hadn't seen much of each other. I'm sure the fact that we settled on opposite coasts had something to do with that.

But there was this too. From the time our paths first crossed, Red had been the most principled man I'd ever met. At the time the trait had seemed totally admirable. Red was, I suppose, more than a friend. He was a hero. It was the Sixties and we'd both opposed the war in Vietnam. I was a goofball. Red was a firebrand. He marched and spoke out. Red opened his own tobacco shop. I attended the grand opening. At first, his big bay window on the avenue was full of pipes and cigars and all other manner of inviting tobacciana. Within six weeks of his grand opening the first pictures of napalmed children made their disturbing appearance in that window. Within six months they'd taken over. A customer would walk into Red's shop, place a two hundred dollar pipe next to the register for payment, casually mention something remotely flattering about Robert McNamara or Richard Nixon, and in the blink of an eye find himself deposited on the sidewalk, pipeless and badly insulted. Only Red seemed oblivious to the fact that such a merchandising strategy almost guaranteed economic calamity. And sure enough, within the year I found myself attending the grand closing of Red's tobacco shop.

Evil smoking pipes, be they beautiful or ugly, play on the mind. I'm thinking now that my disappointing experience with the W.O. has left me to ponder this. In a young man caught up in turbulent times, certain extreme behavior can seem downright admirable. But times change and some people don't. What in a man of thirty may seem principled, can in the same set-in-his-ways man of sixty be a major character flaw. To oppose what is unjust is laudable. To oppose anything and everything across the span of an entire lifetime seems something less. So I sit here now thinking of my old friend Red and the things he missed out on by being him . . . just as I suppose we all miss out on things by being us. And as I tap out the ash from this nasty, for so long unsmoked beautiful pipe, I wish nothing more than that I'd left it in its box.

Different Kettle of Fish

Dud doesn't know from pipes. Dud doesn't wanna know from pipes. All Dud wants to know from is getting high and entertainment wrestling. But Dud's my wife's forty-nine-year-old "kid brother." So when the Battle-Ax From Hell picks me off just as I'm sneaking out the back door and chortles, "Why don't you take Dud along with you, sweetie?" my goose is cooked. All the fun I was hoping to have at the 6th Annual New York Pipe Swap Spectacular is kaput, over and done before I can even step off the stoop.

Truth be told, I'd had a little turnabout in my feeling about going to the pipe show even before I got myself partnered up with my dim-witted brother-in-law. I mean, smoking a pipe in the privacy of one's home is one thing. Bidding on an occasional estate briar on-line is, I suppose, a forgivable proclivity along similar lines. True, both habits are outside the norm. However, they're both private and discreet. But pipe shows are a different kettle of fish altogether.

Don't know what I mean? Well, try thinking of it the way I do. Let's say it's napoleons you like instead of pipes. Yeah, pretend you've got this serious addiction to multi-layered glazed French dessert treats. Every night you find yourself sneaking around behind the patisserie, headlights turned off, praying no one you know spots your car. You buy one napoleon on good nights, two or more on bad ones. And before you turn in after

17

checking to see how many babies have been thrown out how many windows on the late night local news, those sticky treats are always all devoured. Maybe you even subscribe to pastry magazines. You enjoy yourself, perhaps more than you should, looking at risqué pictures of napoleons in varying states of culinary undress. The situation is not an entirely healthy one. But it is, like I say, both private and discreet.

Now imagine yourself getting up early one Saturday morning in December to drive to a giant napoleon festival out by the airport. You shuffle self-consciously through the gliding glass doors of this gigantic eat-fest wishing you were invisible. The sign above the entrance says it all: 6th ANNUAL NAPOLEON EATERS SWAP MEET SPECTACULAR. You plop down ten hard-earned bucks for the privilege of being allowed to go inside and publicly munch napoleons with other napoleon eaters just like yourself. And voila, there you are standing in public, as out of the closet as a man can get with his clothes on. Stretched out before you, wall-to-wall, are folding tables. Every one is strewn with napoleons. There are bent napoleons, straight napoleons, napoleons with smooth and sandblasted glazes. Some of the napoleons come from Italy. Others, the bigger, oddly shaped ones with bumps on top from Scandinavia. Confusingly, because as we all know the napoleon is a French creation, most of the thousands of napoleons being exhibited at the show are stamped "MADE IN ENGLAND."

There is even a table dedicated to nothing but utensils for eating napoleons . . . knives, forks, spoons, and presumably, for those who eat their napoleons on the run and can't be bothered lugging a complete table setting in their breast pocket, a nifty foldout three-way device made in Czechoslovakia. As a napoleon eater you've always known such strange gadgets existed. You accept them as a fact of life. Like most napoleon eaters, you think of your beloved dessert treats the way a Navy man might conjure a carrier group. The napoleon itself is your carrier. The myriad support utensils needed to eat and clean up after it are your destroyers and cruisers. All such naval analogies seem absolutely normal to the napoleon-eating mind.

You find yourself being pushed along by a grasping, murmuring throng of fellow napoleon eaters. Their unbridled enthusiasm has molded them into a human river. There is an actual current in this crowded room. You sense yourself being transformed into a thinking, breathing cork. You bob along from one folding table to the next. At a particularly busy one by the exit, a group of older men hold court. Gray and whiskered, they're bunched in a literal knot of camaraderie that hints at the existence of some secret brotherhood. Then, non-observant creature that you are, you notice they're gathered beneath a large banner of their own making. It clearly identifies them as members of the NEW YORK NAPOLEON CLUB. Apparently, it is these affable fellows who are hawking hats, scarves, tee shirts, baby bibs and religious artifacts with images of napoleons emblazoned upon them. Business at their table seems especially brisk.

At a table adjoining theirs, you notice a man wearing just such a tee shirt. It is inked with a colorful representation of a napoleon that has been unmistakably altered. By some form of photographic alchemy, perhaps photo-shopped manipulation of alternating compressions and expansions, this pastry has most unexpectedly taken on the shape of a buxom woman. In box lettering beneath this mind-boggling image is this query: HEY, BIG BOY . . . ARE YOU MAN ENOUGH FOR ME? And as if all this were not enough, the bill of this same napoleon eater's ball cap is emblazoned with the message, I LIVE TO EAT NAPOLEONS.

This festooned fellow is looking at you as you look at him. You feel as though you are caught in a mirror. The sorry, slightly silly, addicted creature that will not allow your attention to waver reminds you of yourself. You don't want it to be so. But all the wishing in the world can't alter the truth one iota.

Imagine all this, every nightmarish scene just as I've described it. Then you will know what I mean when I say, "Pipe shows are a different kettle of fish altogether."

But like most men, even though I'm condemned to suffer the ridiculous antics of my own imagination, in matters that matter I'm able to ignore them as well. For instance, on this particular morning my need to see pipes trumps all fear of appearing foolish in public. So Dud and I are off to the show in my little Toyota. I'm trying to make small talk with my pipe show copilot, Dud. But he's sitting shotgun, silent as a stone. Now from where Dud and I live, the road to Newark takes you down the New Jersey Turnpike. And if you've ever driven it, I don't have to tell you that the Jersey Turnpike is one savage road. Cutting across the Great Secaucus marshlands, its path is pocked with swamp gas, standing waters, and flames like dragon's breath belching from industrial chimneys ten stories high. If the very worst sort of giants lived beneath the primordial muck of this place, chimneys like these would be their middle fingers, rude digits poking up into the eye of a machine-gray sky of their own making. No doubt about it. The Pike's got Dud spooked. To himself as much as me, he's mumbling under his breath. "Faster man, faster. Get me outta here." For a pleasant change, now it's me who's got nothing to say to him.

We dive off the Turnpike at Exit 14. Things get dramatically worse. We've called ahead for directions, and been instructed by a mechanical voice on a scratchy phone machine to simply "stay right at the exit and you can't get lost." And surprise, surprise, we've been lied to. Dud and I have done exactly as told. We've navigated loops and flyovers and traversed a couple of trestle bridges that led us to a railroad yard with rats big as longshoremen. We even got ourselves hopelessly lost in a doomsday neighborhood where smirking mothers pushed baby carriages with automatic weapons slung across their grotesquely humped backs.

Now we're back at the very same toll booth for a third go-round, hoping against hope that the obscenely overpaid state employee who's already lied to us twice for his own sick amusement is not still up to his old tricks. And Dud is bawling like a baby, begging the way a man begs when he thinks his very life may hang in the balance. This comedic undertaker of a toll man is ignoring Dud. He's addressing me in the slow, overly respectful, completely indifferent tone civil servants love to affect. It's that easily recognizable inflection the human voice assumes when it gets pinched down to a "go fuck yourself" whisper by the application of tax dollars at work! "Now, sir, as I've tried to tell you twice already, it is very, very simple . . ." And to Dud and me it is all just a dreadful drone, sounds that do not quite make words, words that don't make sentences, an audible warning signal that what is simple to one man can be impossible to another. That out in the no-man's land of the Jersey Turnpike, one man's dream is usually another's nightmare.

We adapt. We navigate. We arrive. At the hotel Dud takes one final, long toke on a cuffed joint. I slip one of my expendable pipes into his shirt pocket and instruct him to "stay close and do as I do."

At a table laden with multi-thousand dollar freehands, a Danish gentleman engages us in casual conversation. The room is smoke-free. It's Jersey law. You can feel the mega-anxiety mandatory abstention has placed on this Danish gentleman and the room at large. No one is mentioning it. As if by mutual assent it seems not to be a topic of conversation in the room. But I have this theory. It says pipe smokers—myself first and foremost—are braves of a strange tribe. I contend that if you place me in a room with ten men, one of which is a fellow pipe smoker, and simply leave us to make chit-chat, I will within ten minutes know with biblical certainty the identity of the mystery smoker.

Now I say this knowing full-well that feats of profiling are not looked on with favor in modern day America—especially on and about the Jersey Turnpike! So I will stop short of telling you what traits I look for to perform my trick. Perhaps, at a later date when we know each other better, we might make such revelations the topic of a separate, private conversation. But I will tell you this. Every one of those quirky character anomalies that tend to give a pipe smoker away is only exacerbated by the absence of a pipe in his hand and smoke in his mouth. Why, one could no more misidentify a room full of pipe smokers simply because they are not chewing stems and blowing smoke, than take a ride on the Orient Express with the New York Philharmonic sans instruments and not know you were in the presence of musical genius.

So take my word for it. There was a palpable stress you could feel pressing down on this room crowded with pipe swappers long before Dud began gagging violently and falling to the floor. The cause seemed to have been a fistful of smokeless chewing tobacco offered up by the Danish gentleman to both Dud and me. We'd both accepted the unfamiliar wads in good faith, Dud, no doubt, in remembrance of my admonition to "stay close and do as I do." But I'd accepted a small pinch, Dud apparently much more. I chewed mine. He'd attempted to swallow his. White foam speckled with small bits of a darker substance I assumed in the ensuing hubbub to be mint-flavored plug tobacco began issuing from Dud's frothing mouth.

There he lay, the poor, trusting, stoned wretch, the violent jerking motions of his prostrate torso half-hidden by a folding table littered high with ten dollar estate pipes jumbled one atop another in tattered orange crates. Dud's tragicomic appearance precluded, I suppose, any serious effort by anyone at mouth-to-mouth resuscitation. But fortunately for Dud, his powers of self-recovery proved remarkable. If a referee had been present to mark his fall, I suppose Dud might just have beaten the man's count to ten.

But public fuss is not what a pipe show is all about. Pipemen are famously proud of their powers of controlled reserve, their ability not to cause a rumpus even in the worst of circumstance. What did old Alf Dunhill call it? "The gentle art of pipe smoking." And this, what happened to Dud, was anything but gentle. So although no one asked us to, having literally just arrived, Dud and I now hightailed it for the exit.

I'd hoped to have time to meet a few pipe luminaries. Maybe even fill my bowl with a pinch or two of interesting-sounding tobacco. One that for sure caught my eye was called TEN RUSSIANS. The sample tin had, inexplicably, not a single Russian on it. The singular figure on the label was a bedraggled sea captain, the helmsman's wheel in his hand. I stared at this label, performing a mini-study of this seaman's eyes and features. I became convinced he was no more a Russian than I was. Somehow, this visual anomaly made me want to sample the coal black strands of tobacco in that tin more than ever. And now, thanks to Dud and his unsightly antics, I supposed my little investigation into those nowhere-to-be-seen ten Russians and their dark, yummy tobacco would have to wait for another day.

"... *trestle bridges that led us to a railroad yard with rats big as longshoremen.*"

How I Smoke In Public (And Get Away With It)

I apologize to no one. I ask no man's permission. I do not take my pipe out and place it on a table unless I fully intend to smoke it. That is what I do. I am, after all, a pipe smoker. I follow the Pipe Smoker Way. I live by my wits and the force of my determination. If I suspect I am in hostile territory, surrounded by anti-smoking thugs, I forgive them their anti-smoking ways. I do not ask them to leave the room whenever I decide to fire up, and I good-naturedly ignore their entreaties for me to do likewise. And I do have my bag of tricks.

The first thing I do if planning to smoke in public is snatch up my custom, self-carved smoking-in-public pipe. It is carved from REAL BRIAR and shaped like an old-fashioned phone receiver, the one with the handle in the middle and the talking and listening cups at either end. The talking end of my smoking in public pipe is a cleverly disguised pipe mouthpiece. The listening end, the cup against which one might be expected to place one's ear, is a bowl. And the handle portion between the two is in reality . . . you guessed it . . . a pipe stem! How freaking clever is that? And when I wish to smoke in public I simply go, "bring, bring, bring" loud enough for everyone to hear. And I just light that baby up right at the dining table, yummy tobacco smoke pouring from my ear and from my mouth. And when some busybody anti-smoking thug accuses me of smoking in public and asks me to put out my pipe/phone, I reply, "Sorry, but I'm on a very important overseas call and I'm not at liberty to hang up."

For those pipe smokers lacking the huge appendages necessary to pull this very public, never fails performance off, I've got a few more recommended tricks up the old sleeve. If you're in proximity to a stove you might want to try this one. Carve yourself, from REAL BRIAR of course, a giant oom paul in the exact shape of a kitchen ladle. Then, when you feel the urge to fire up, place your back to the anti-smoking thugs in the kitchen and draw that match over the spoon-shaped end of your "ladle," which is really . . . you guessed it . . . a pipe bowl. Now bend down low over whatever happens to be cooking at the moment and pretend to stir it with your "ladle," all the while puffing on it like a madman. With dense black clouds of latikia smoke pouring from your smiling mouth and nostrils, counter the outrage of your host and fellow kitchen company by responding, "Yum-yum. I think this (and here you might insert the name of whatever happens to be cooking in the pot you've just been pretending to stir) is almost done."

And finally, there is this ditty. It takes practice. But like all my methods, it works every time. Not many people outside the medical profession know this, but the human diaphragm is a two-way pump. It pushes both up and down. So here's what you do. You cuff your little self-carved pipe made from REAL BRIAR in your palm and draw it casually over the candles ablaze at the dining table. Now, with all that yummy English tobacco invisibly crackling inside your down-turned palm, pretend to cough. The fake cough is a complete ruse, your excuse to inhale unnoticed by the anti-smoking thugs at the table. So far, so good. But now your problem is what to do with the inhaled smoke. Blow it out and the jig is up. But here's what you do. Use that talented, practiced diaphragm of yours to blow all that yummy pipe smoke down into your abdomen rather than up. It will now pass pleasantly from your body from a most unexpected orifice. And if someone does happen to notice you are now sitting on a cloud of reprehensible tobacco smoke, simply whisper, "You simply must forgive me. I seem to have the most terrible gas."

The Island of Dr. Moreau

My brother-in-law, Dud, operates on the outer fringes of the Briar Brotherhood. Much of the smoking he does traditionally involves metal screens or small pieces of perforated aluminum foil stuffed down inside the gurgling bowls of battered little pipes. But he can be a bit of a pipe snob when the mood is upon him. Sometimes I'll come home from a hard day's work at the tar pits to find Dud decked out in my snazzy twin-breasted smoking jacket, feet up in my La-Z-Boy, watching wide-screen and puffing one of my prized briars.

It's not like Dud doesn't have a pipe or two of his own. Over the years the wife and I have gifted him more than a few. Nothing extravagant or particularly special, mind you . . . a few Ben Wade freehands with plateau tops, a GBD Rockroot Canadian with a cracked shank, two full-bent Dr. Plumbs, one smooth and one rusticated, even a small calabash with a scorched meerschaum bowl and a stem chewed nearly in half. But wouldn't you know it? Dud won't smoke a one of them. Oh no, my brother-in-law would rather go through my three-tiered Decatur rack and pick out one of my priceless collector pieces to mishandle.

I tolerate this. As incomprehensible as it seems, I sit by and say nothing as I watch my Group 5 Dunhill Root finish six-panel turned into a hash pipe, my Savinelli Autograph savaged for the consumption of stinky cannabis. You ask why, and I'll tell you . . . because in all the world there's nothing more fearsome than a wife on the rampage. One word of recrimination from me directed at my wife's "baby brother" and I've got World War III on my hands. A single unkind syllable and home-cooked meals as I've known them become a culinary memory. The merest suggestion on my part that my slovenly, freeloading live-in relative give a care for my property, and any and all hope I may still be harboring of ever experiencing partnered sex one last time before I die goes up in smoke. These, it would seem, are the terms of my marital existence.

And now, on top of all that, there is this as well. Saturday I came in from raking leaves to find Dud supine in my recliner, my Comoy churchwarden Christmas pipe clenched in his visibly unbrushed teeth, a copy of the Pipe Collector in his hand. "You know," he says to me, "I think this fellow Newcombe just might be on to something here. This whole idea about boring out the stems and shanks of smoking pipes just makes good sense." Two simple, clearly enunciated declarative sentences fashioned in the King's best English, and I heard not a word. How is that possible, you ask? Well, it's because, in truth, I never listen to Dud. Haven't for years. And strange as it sounds, I don't fault myself for that. It's a matter of self-preservation. You simply cannot live with a moron for years and not tune him out. It just can't be done. The alternative, as I see it, is gradual but inevitable brain damage.

So a statement that should have served as a flashing red warning signal went unheeded. As a consequence, last evening I came home to find my entire collection of pipes, more than a hundred high-end beauties, scattered carelessly about the kitchen counters. Each and every one of them had been stabbed through. And when I say "stabbed through" I mean just that, stabbed through end-to-end, pierced down the shank and out the bowl in the exact same way a drunken nautical man might go about scuttling his dingy. Dud's weapon of choice had been a 5/32nds titanium drill bit hitched to the business end of a T-handle tap wrench, the very instrument recommended by Mr. Rick Newcombe in his well-intentioned article in the Pipe Collector on how best to enlarge the airways in troublesome briars.

Unaccountably, every fail-safe mechanism that might have saved me from such a catastrophe had failed. The no doubt well-intentioned clerk at my local True Value hardware store had, in the distracting hubbub of his busy sales day, apparently mistaken my brother-in-law for just one more normal, clear-thinking customer and not the dangerous menace he is. In an effort to do exactly what he is paid to do—be helpful—I can only assume the young sales chap listened to Dud's entreaties concerning the need for certain tools to do a certain job. And in response he'd done what must have seemed his professional duty. He'd placed in my brother-in-law's diabolical hands a six-inch long, aviation-style, twist drill. Well, he may as well have sold whisky to Indians, a 45 revolver and a box of hollow point shells to the Son of Sam. As a player of chess might say, the young clerk could not see far enough into his position to see the danger ahead. What minimum wage, barely out of high school kid in a checkered vest could?

The choreographed ballet of error and missed opportunity this retail oversight began has culminated in the total destruction of my entire pipe collection. A treasure assembled over the course of a lifetime has been turned to junk in a day. For Dud took his razor-sharp, six-inch long dagger of mass destruction home and rammed it clean through every four-and-a-half inch long pipe I own. In doing so he pierced the lovingly polished underbellies of severely hooked oom pauls and graceful bents. Into the stiff-upper-lip face of ramrod straight billiards, Dublins and pots alike, Dud added a gapping cleft to the chin.

For as long as I can remember, within the briar fraternity a debate has raged as to whether grain patterns affect smoking properties. Sadly, on this question I have no wisdom to impart. But this I can tell you. Birdseye and straight grain alike lack the structural integrity to resist the metallic twistings and pokings of a mindless brother-in-law. Down the shanks, across the bowls and out the outer walls his whirling weapon came, methodically popping perfectly round 5/32nds wide little mouse holes in both grains alike.

And still, as if all this were not enough, the simple drilling of holes where one would devoutly wish no holes to be does not sound the seemingly unfathomable depths of my brother-in-law's depravity. I believe even Dud, in the innermost recesses of his by now largely addled mind must have sensed the line between acceptable civil behavior and wonton anarchy had been crossed. Surely the blows I rained down upon his face and torso must have had some effect. For tonight I've returned home to find this. By way of amends, I suppose, Dud has been at it again. Again my once precious pipes are scattered across kitchen counters like so much dirty silverware. And to my amazement, what I'm witnessing is this. Over each pipe's unnecessary hole a foreign object has been Crazy Glued. No two objects are alike. Sticking out the bottoms and sides of one cluster of briars I recognize the pieces from the deluxe Monopoly game I'd all but forgotten in the hall closet. Another cluster is "mended" with old pennies and dimes and nickels pirated from the change drawer. Even some of the smaller cars and trucks my toddler son just yesterday so enjoyed pushing over the smooth tiles of our kitchen floor are now integral and attached parts of my pipe collection.

Why, here is one of my favorite pipes, a Victorian era silver-banded Barling with a deep bend and an almost calabash-shaped bowl. I spent a small fortune winning that baby on eBay. To this day I've never seen its like. Tonight, to my surprise, the decorative little ball at the uppermost tip of my wife's holiday saltshaker has been inserted into its circular wound. The open end of the perforated silver salt cone that would normally screw onto the shaker now faces downward, and to my amazement, when I set it down I discover my beloved Victorian Barling has overnight become a sitter pipe.

Make no mistake. What I'm looking at and describing is grotesque. I wouldn't recommend these Island of Dr. Moreau pipes, monstrosities really, half briar and half Tonka toy, on the collection of my worst enemy. Still, when I think of how much effort poor, stupid Dud has put into this fix-'em-up plan of his, how can I stay mad at him? And besides, bad as my pipes look with all these ridiculous trinkets sticking out the sides and bottoms of their bowls, I guess at least now they're smokeable again. Now, all I've gotta do is figure out how I'm gonna get these briar oddities back in their racks. All those smooth little spoon-shaped indentations into which they once slid so effortlessly are never gonna accept the jagged geometry of little metal shoes and top hats. I think we can all agree it's an interesting dilemma I've got on my hands. Anyone out there got any creative solutions to suggest?

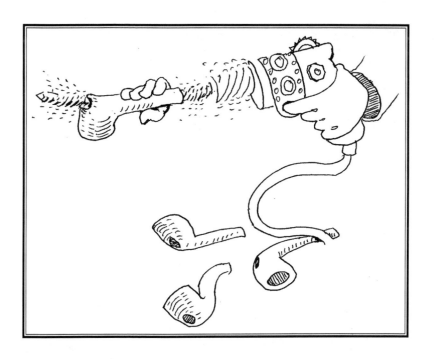

"Down the shanks, across the bowls and out the outer walls
his whirling weapon came."

The U-Boat Skipper's GBD

I have an unnatural affinity for used pipes that come with stories attached. Most such vintage smoking instruments tend to be dark and oily. To me, having patina on a pipe is like whiskers on a man's face. Both come with age. Both provide character. So when it comes to my pipes, yes, I like them dark and oily. But color is not the primary thing that draws me to an estate pipe. The dull brown sheen of worn hazel nut that many old-timer pipes acquire through repeated handlings is but the "X" on a treasure map to me. It marks the spot where the treasure I seek might be hidden. And that treasure is the pipe's story.

If an eBay solicitation states, "these pipes belonged to my grandfather," sight unseen I'm already half-crazed to close the deal. If another ad should say "this GBD pipe was smoked by my mother's grandfather while he was fighting in WWII (German side, I'm afraid)," and that particular pot should have an original stem with the little metal GBD logo intact and the button literally chewed off by tooth chatter caused by a hundred fathoms of depth-charge angst, well, then if it's within my financial power (or without and my wife can be kept from knowing), that pipe's coming home to me.

And the stories in my collection do not end with a purchase. Because for each pipe with a tale I snare on eBay, I send a follow-up letter to the seller, soliciting any and all additional information they can provide about my newest acquisition. Sure. A few sellers turn out to be dealers, spinners of yarns, clever merchandisers who've no doubt heard of the existence of strange collector creatures like myself, and simply make it up as they go along as a means of spurring interest. But a high percentage of eBay sellers I've dealt with are the Real McCoy, and when family information is available, it is usually forthcoming.

Turns out my German submariner with the nervous teeth did not survive the war. Before his final, fatal voyage he'd put his pipe in dry dock for repairs. God only knows what got fixed, because when it arrived at my home seventy-some odd years after the fact, the stem was still perforated, top and bottom, and the cake on that naval veteran was still a good quarter inch thick. If ghost tastes can be trusted to tell the truth, I figured it to have been built up mostly of English tobacco residue. Funny that . . . the image of a German submariner holding an English pipe full of English tobacco in one hand, while with the other he's pushing whooshing torpedo buttons sending British merchantmen to Davy Jones' Locker. But whatever those mystery repairs might have been, this particular U-boat skipper for sure would have been better off staying on land himself and sending his pipe on that final, ill-fated voyage. Oh, if only the future was there for us to see in advance!

Be all that as it may, my larger point is this. Most people are anxious to share their family stories. They'll pour out the most private details simply for the asking. And pipes with stories like these infinitely enrich the pleasure I get from sitting back and firing up these small pieces of briar history. Because as any sensitive collector of pipes knows, the pipe cradled in one's hand at the end of another savage work day is more, much more than simply a piece of carved wood. If a pipe is loved, in time it will become an extension of its owner.

Yes, a good pipe can be all of that and more. To me, the best smokers in my rack are high priests, best friends, trusted confessors who share my most peaceful and private thoughts. And to others, the largely hostile non-smoking world, these same pipes hint at all the unspoken things I'd never dream of saying aloud about myself. Now how many inanimate objects can lay claim to being all of that? And even after such a pipe has passed into new hands—through happy or sad circumstance—a part of their former owner moves forward as well. And when such a pipe is lit, and if you know how it's done, then each and every smoke you share with that pipe allows you to channel all that pipe's previous masters. And the more you know about that person, the easier this mystifying process becomes.

Past masters run the gamut from doomed sailors to heads of state. Another of my treasures, a big, silver-mounted bent cryptically stamped "VPHN erikas" along its dark and oily shank, came to me as "owned by my great-grandfather, who served in the American diplomatic service during the Great War." In a written follow-up to my post-purchase inquiry, it turns out this great-grandfather split time after the war between Paris and Berlin. He'd met the woman who would become his wife in Paris. Perhaps, way before thinking of herself as someone's wife, much less some unborn pipe smoker's great grandmother, this thoughtful woman had gone out on the occasion of her beau's birthday. She'd shopped in a Paris that still belonged to Hemingway and Joyce and Picasso and a thousand other free spirits. And she'd gotten her lucky man this bird's-eyed gem of a pipe. I know it sounds strange to those who've never experienced it, but I swear I can feel this long-dead woman's generosity in each and every puff of that great smoking pipe.

". . . a German submariner holding an English pipe full
of English tobacco in one hand, while with the other
he's pushing whooshing torpedo buttons sending British
merchantmen to Davy Jones' Locker."

Am I Alone Here, People?

You gotta hand it to Old Alf Dunhill. The man was a marketing genius. I mean, the man didn't exactly invent red pipe stain. But he was the first guy with the business savvy to give all those rosy-cheeked pipes a marketable name, "Bruyere." And what a confounding name it is! Am I alone here, people, in thinking Bruyere sounds like a particularly foreign word for smelly French cheese? Maybe that's part of why I'm so disinclined toward red pipes. Big fan of light walnut though, the shade Old Alf the naming genius christened "Root." Root's the Abe Lincoln of pipe stains. It can't tell a lie. No hiding flaws and fills with light walnut. And it does for shapely briar grain exactly what the small black cocktail dress does for attractive women. It shows them off to advantage. So for sure, when it comes to pipes, make mine light walnut every time.

The pipe I've just finished smoking is a Barling lumberman. It has a wide oval shank I find particularly sexy. Unfortunately, it is smeared all over with stain the hideous purple of castle drapes and nine out of ten Victorian settees. It's the very hue of coagulating blood this pipeman associates with Dunhill Bruyere and smelly French cheese. And that's not the all of it. Another issue I have with this Barling is its finish. If I were a house paint color chart, which I emphatically am not, I'd describe this pipe as high gloss. If it weren't a Barling, I'd suspect some factory nincompoop of having dropped it in a vat of lacquer. As it is, it being an eBay acquisition, I suppose the previous owner/

seller simply assumed several ounces of beeswax globbed on the outside of the bowl might attract a few extra bidders.

Am I alone here, people, in wishing sellers of estate pipes would simply leave the old wood alone? I mean, since when did a nice flat patina and a nickel's worth of hard-crusted cake become badges of shame on used briar? Why must every pipe in the world look just as it did when it first jumped out the box? Aren't there enough actual new pipes out there looking just like new to go around? I, for one, say leave the old pipes alone. To me, a hundred-year-old pipe in high shine is the briar equivalent of a bald guy with a dead raccoon for a wig. I ask you: what's so outrageous about expecting both pipes and people to look their age?

So let's see. So far this Barling lumberman has, for me anyway, the wrong color and wrong finish. And to complete the negative trifecta, its nomenclature couldn't be more damning. The word "Barling" stamped atop that sexy oval shank is scripted when we all know the gold standard for old Barlings is block print. And as pipe guys I don't have to tell you what that means, right? This ruby red loser of a pipe is post-transition, non-family, or as Richard Carelton Hacker puts it so cold-bloodedly in his classic book on the older wood, this baby is "of no collector interest." Color, finish, pedigree, everything wrong as wrong can be. A real three-strikes-and-you're-out pipe, right?

But somehow, owing to some pipemaker's miracle, this Barling is the best smoker in my collection. Nothing else in my well-stocked racks compares to it. All the well-heeled and dearly priced Charatans, Castellos, Ashtons, Dunhills, and Sasienis can stay in the firehouse when the fire whistle blows around here, because this mutt of a Barling out-smokes them all, hands down. Put a match to this baby and it fires up rim-to-rim without needing a charring light. It smokes as if synchronized to my respiration. Never a need to rush with this Barling. Put it down. Walk away. Take a leak. Grab a snack from the frig. Make love to the old lady! Come back and it's still smoldering, the gentlest wisp of tobacco smoke crowning the rim of the bowl the way a warm morning mist blankets a cool lake on a perfect fishing morning. Inhale and down goes that pleasant mist through all those tasty strands of tobacco, down and out in one long, delicious, lazy stream of pure smoky satisfaction. The perfect puff!

So here is my question. How can a pipe with so much going against it be so good? What makes one unlikely pipe more perfect than all others? Last time I herded my collection together in one place for a proper count, I owned upwards of a hundred head of pipes (I know, that's a no-no, no such thing as a herd or head of pipes—but analogies pushed to ridiculous lengths appeal to my abnormal sense of humor and I am the writer here). Of that hundred, perhaps five of them possess some degree of an intangible quality it pleases me at this moment to call "magical smokability." Now I don't spend tons of cash on my pipes. I'm gonna guess my average estate pipe sets me back anywhere between twenty and forty bucks a pop. So in that squalid price neighborhood, with a little bit of buying savvy and average luck, I'm guessing approximately one in twenty pipes purchased has an outside chance of turning out to be a "magical smoker."

I have no way of knowing this, but I'm gonna guess if I could pay more, buy better, this ratio of new (to me) used pipe to great smoker would grow ever closer to a one-to-one ratio. From what I read in my pipe magazines and this newsletter, it seems reasonable to think so. I've yet to find a single article in one of them where one of the stalwarts of our hobby has purchased an expensive handmade and found it to smoke even remotely like a rat. And if the truth were otherwise, I suppose it would never be known. The fortunate few who can afford multi-hundred dollar "art pipes" can not be forced to testify against themselves in print. Human nature is human nature. Am I alone here, people, in supposing spending a thousand dollars or more on a single smoking instrument is to convince oneself in advance that the pipe in question can only be a great smoker?

But tell me this if you can. Most pipe reviewers put the smoking differential between pipes up to one of two things. First is the briar itself. Is it Corsican, Algerian, Greek, Spanish? How has it been cured—air, oil, heat? And for how long? The second is engineering. How well is the pipe designed? What shape is the burn chamber, the thickness of the walls? And then there is that most recent bone of contention, the gnarly one that swirls around the size and evenness of the bore and its relationship to the bottom of the bowl. Humble pipemen everywhere who are just happy to have a pipe and afford tobacco are being alerted to the fact that if the bore is too closed on our humble briars, an overworking condition can result and grossly affect our pleasure. Excess heat builds up. Taste suffers.

Pipe smoking peace of mind goes out the window. Suddenly, overnight, millions of pipe smokers who've for a lifetime only known the business end of our pipes, the big end where we carelessly jam in tobacco and apply the match, find ourselves peeking for the first time ever down that little hole in the button. Am I alone here, people, in feeling a bit unnatural doing this? And yes, a bit dirty as well, leering down an orifice that was for so long both private and unobserved?

And for what purpose? To what end? Where is the reason in such perverse activity? I mean, I have one pipe, a charter member of my Fab Five, that is a supreme smoker, a Tom Turkey among hens. It passes an extra thick pipe cleaner without so much as rumpling the nap. Another of my go-to smoking champs requires me to don exercise gear and break a sweat just getting a bristly thin guy halfway up its stem. These two pipes are identical twins in smokability and unrecognizable one from the other in matters of bore and openness. I see no pattern here that allows me to draw any conclusion whatsoever about how opening the draft on any particular pipe might affect its smokability. So again I ask, why must the smoking of some pipes always be a labor of love, while the smoking of the magical few is always no labor at all?

Zen Buddhists believe—and here I'm winging it because I am no Zen Buddhist—one must learn all there is to know about enlightenment from a great teacher—or on-line, I suppose, if a qualified guru is not to be found in your neck of the woods—and then, if you really want to climb down from that exhausting Cycle of Life, forget all you have learned. You see, in Zen Buddhism it's never information that sets you free. The key to Nirvana is the wisdom to set all worldly information aside, which of course can only be done once you've acquired it. Don't know about the rest of you, but I feel much the same way about our beloved hobby, the smoking and collecting of pipes. Once you've absorbed all the experts have to say about the small hole at the skinny end of your pipe, you must endeavor to forget it. We must forsake all worldly knowledge of the little hole in order to regain the blissful ignorance of our pipe smoking grandfathers, those puffing savages whose interest in their pipes began and ended at the big end, the one into which they clumsily jammed tobacco. Am I alone here, people, in believing this?

Small Life

Old-time New Yorkers will tell you how the West Side Highway once ran uninterrupted all the way from the GWB in the north down to the Brooklyn Battery Tunnel at its southernmost tip. Traffic permitting, in those days you could scamper like a naughty mouse on a sleeping lady's leg from one end of Manhattan Island to the other without encountering a single traffic light. Those were the days, and those days are gone.

I remember the black-and-white news shot that signaled the end of the era. For decades cobblestones had been falling out of that neglected roadway, bread loaf-sized chunks of granite shed like chiseled tears for a once great city grown too poor and too indifferent to maintain its own roads. Deterioration was at its worst down below 57th Street in the elevated section that ran alongside the piers. Along that bustling stretch the proud ocean liners of the day would submit themselves to the indignity of being tugged to berth after battering days at sea, their long, painted flanks lashed fast to slimy pilings with coiled rope thick as a longshoreman's forearm. The tall black stacks of those maritime behemoths would be on display to the wondering eyes of small children held captive in the back seats of their parents' vibrating cars, vulcanized rubber tires set to jitterbugging on a washboard of rapidly disintegrating roadway.

And then, one day, right there on the front page of the Daily News, there it was, the gravity-defying news photo of somebody's family roadster dangling like the cantered pendulum of a broken clock from its rear wheels in the mother of all potholes, its battered hood pointing straight down, a good thirty feet above 12th Avenue. Cheaper, one supposes, to tear down than repair, within a year the elevated roadway was gone—gone the way of steel that rusts and cement that cracks and a city's dreams that shatter of ever becoming the New Rome.

These days, for all practical purposes, the once great West Side Highway has been cut in half, squeezed down like a toothpaste tube and dribbled out onto city streets at 57th Street. One moment you're flying along on a highway that seems almost commensurate with the colossal conceits of the city that built it. Everything that moves in Manhattan being "traffic permitting," you're zipping south past the terraced parks of Washington Heights and Harlem. The awe-catching spires of Riverside Church and Grant's Tomb fill your rearview. Out the passenger window the misleading sparkle of the Hudson River and that bobbing monument to obscene opulence, the moored yachts of the 79th Street Boat Basin, pass in a blur.

And then, suddenly there's nothing ahead but an off-ramp. And as quickly as that, any and all pretense of metropolitan majesty dies with the sunlight. You've been ejected onto the dark, seedy wharfiness of 12th Avenue, set loose in a funhouse from hell of mind-numbingly slow and inexplicably unsynchronized traffic lights.

My story begins there, at the corner of 57th Street and 12th Avenue. Well, not exactly there, because the 57th Street terminus of the West Side Highway dumps you down onto 12th Avenue at 52nd Street. Now seventy years ago 52nd Street was an address city-goers came in search of. The most famous jazz clubs in Manhattan north of the Greenwich Village mews electrified 52nd Street with their gaudy marquee lights. If you wanted to see Monk or Bird or Miles, you came to 52nd Street. But those clubs are long gone.

These days nobody that doesn't live or work on 52nd Street wants anything to do with that congested block. 57th Street is the main East-West artery motorists seek now. Follow it up the hill away from the river and it takes you to Columbus Circle and the southernmost gate of Central Park. You're a short walk from Lincoln Center. But to get there from the West Side Highway, for reasons Robert Moses took to his grave, you've gotta come five blocks too far south, make a U-turn on 12th Avenue, and then travel back north to 57th.

Back in the day when my story is taking place, the mid-Sixties, you did all this seemingly unnecessary maneuvering in a really bad neighborhood. In the inky blackness of city night, the abandoned warehouses and chained-closed piers that lined those godforsaken few blocks may as well have been the unwelcoming gates of Count Dracula's castle. And I'm nineteen and I'm alone and I'm sitting in my sputtering jalopy at maybe three in the morning, waiting for the interminable light at the pitch black corner of 57th and 12th to go green. I've got this urgent need to turn right and escape up that long hill running away from the river before my lumpy engine stalls and my eternal soul is lost forever.

And out of the corner of my eye, to my right, coming down the ramp of what appears to be an abandoned parking garage, I catch a glimpse of this filthy Viking-like creature staggering my way. His hands are raised above his head. He's clearly straining to hold something staggeringly heavy aloft, but for the life of me I can't make out what it is. My attention is shifting in fits and starts between the damn light that won't change and this advancing, menacing apparition. He's coming and the light is not turning, and now he's standing in the middle of the road, directly in front of my car, every unclean inch of him eerily animated by the shadowed glare of my headlights.

The filthy fellow is attired in what appears to be the mottled skin of a diseased buffalo. Atop a wild mop of matted hair is a horned helmet fashioned from what appeared to be battered hubcaps. The only part of his face not blacken enough with soot to absorb all light are two wild, darting animal eyes. And now I see clearly that this thing he's gone to such pains to keep balanced above his bearded head, the menacing cube suspended directly above the hood of my sputtering car, is a cinder block.

Prevented from running the light by this hulking human figure towering at my front bumper, I recall giving my hands permission to release their death-grip on the steering wheel. With a strange sense of calm I simply sat and watched. Watched as the cinder block hurtled down, not onto me or my car, thank goodness, but the roadway just inches ahead of my front wheels. Then, apparently having done everything he'd felt compelled to do, this Viking-like creature simply pivoted to his side and began retracing his giant's steps back to whence he'd come. In the meanwhile, finally, the cursed light turned green. But my car remained motionless. Having stayed for this much of the riveting production, now, even with a color-coded blessing to legally proceed, I felt compelled to stay, to see this real life horror flick through to its final rolling credits. My final glimpse of my tormentor was as he disappeared by degrees from the feet up down the ramp of his abandoned parking garage home, a water-bloated city rat wobbling unsteadily along by his side.

That memorable night in Manhattan is what, maybe fifty years come and gone? But I still think about it now and again. For a time there I'd all but convinced myself that it had been a show. Think about it. You're an out-of-towner and you've just planted the wheels of your rented car on the vaunted streets of Manhattan. Oh, you've watched stories on Hick Town Evening News about how dangerous those streets are. You've heard all the horror stories. And now, in the space of a few blocks, even before your Big Apple vacation has really gotten rolling, all those stories have come true. I don't know about you, but whenever life starts exceeding my expectations I get suspicious. It's been my experience that boring old real life just doesn't work that way.

So isn't it at least possible, I'm thinking, that this Viking chap was in actuality an employee of the city of New York, a professional actor paid to give wary travelers a mega-dose of everything they fear most? A show on Broadway and dinner at a four-star bistro costs what, maybe five hundred bucks? But a good true horror story to tell all the folks back home, how much might that be worth? My guess is it would be priceless.

And there's this I think about too. Although you don't think about it at the time, for people like myself, ordinary guys living small, ordinary lives, confrontations with filthy urban Vikings are about as big a deal as it gets. One day you find yourself old and looking back, and you realize the stories you've got are the only ones you're going to have, and one of them is this one. And while it was happening it seemed like a distraction, a delay on the way to someone or someplace else you'd hoped might be memorable. But in fact, those minutes spent at that traffic light were your big moment, one of the big times of your small, ordinary life.

And if you've been born with even average intelligence and are blessed with enough time to dope this all out, well, then maybe you devise yourself a strategy for living in the moment, for catching and appreciating your "story moments" as they are occurring. So each time I sit down in my favorite chair to light up one of my favorite smoking pipes with the Corona Big Boy lighter my big-hearted son bought me for Father's Day, I think about all of this. And I approach every puff on every pipe as if it might be one of my big moments, one of the "story moments" of my small, ordinary, happy life.

"*somebody's roadster dangling like the cantered pendulum of a broken clock by its rear wheels in the mother of all potholes.*"

The King Kong of Cake

It's roads that draw me down to Pigeon Forge each autumn. You see, when I'm doing one of the three things I enjoy most and I'm not smoking my pipes and I'm not in bed with the wife, well, then you'll find me out on my motorcycle. And the best damn twisty roads within a short vacation's ride of my home are up the Smoky Mountains, clustered along a squiggly map line separating western North Carolina from eastern Tennessee. Back in the day this was moonshine country, a blessed wild spot on God's green planet where surly guys with souped-up jalopies and trunks fulla hooch could put their skills as wheelmen to the test, leading pesky revenuers on a merry chase down snaking roads that would turn Mario Andretti's hair white with fright.

Those rough boys and their blacked-out road rockets are gone now. Yesterday's sour mash and bathtub gin are today's micro-brews and flavored vodkas. And nowadays, even up here in these outlaw mountains, booze gets delivered in slow moving trucks with polished bumpers and clattering pull-up tailgates. Ungainly as elephant ballerinas, these movable chicanes slow to a pathetic crawl attempting to maneuver their centipede-like wheels around a maddening succession of switchbacks and esses.

Now don't get me wrong. If motorcyclists have a bone to pick, it's with the messenger, not the message. Bikers as a rule love alcohol like doggies love their bones. But they despise the trucks that deliver it much the way brides hate cold sores. These lumbering behemoths block our roads and break the rhythm of our morning rides. Ask anyone on two wheels. They'll tell you. Big rigs have no business clogging up twisty roads. Except, of course, on rainy days. 'Cause when it rains and things get slick on a ribbon of blacktop barely navigable in bright sunshine, on those dark funereal days bikers gotta look for alternate forms of recreation that don't involve two-wheeling.

Which is exactly how I stumbled upon Ike's. Out on one of our "waiting for the weather to clear" reconnaissance missions in a rented car, we spotted a listing old hulk of a general store set back off the road at the end of a gravel drive. Porched on three sides and crowned in rusty tin from eave to eave, its battered screen door pulled against a tired spring that squeaked like a mouse in labor. Inside, a wallow worn into the rough-hewn floor by the boots of time's army wound up and down several short aisles, its serpentine way ending before a cash register that cha-chinged each time its cash drawer popped open. In the back, behind rickety shelving cluttered with pet food, Kotex and other sundry staples, a chipped and faded Coca-Cola cooler slumbered against the wall. Its massive chrome split-lid hinged upward at the center, falling back upon itself with the no-nonsense thump of an ice cream parlor box, inviting the thirsty to reach down and pluck up a frosty soda from a watery bed of ice. Then, with the fist-sized opener screwed fast to the face of the chest, you pushed down on the bottom of your bottle, snapping its cap off with an effervescent "hiss."

Across from that fire-engine-red relic, in a dusty corner I'm sure no human had explored since the days when televisions still sported rabbit ears and gentlemen held doors for ladies, I spied a plastic monstrosity that looked for all the world like a wide-mouthed butter tub on steroids. The snap-up lid on the thing was the size of a hubcap. Bigger than a coal scuttle and smaller than a half keg of beer, in a fisherman's dream such a canister might contain a lifetime supply of night crawlers. But a yellowed label put all misunderstanding to rest. In bold block lettering above a cartoonish figure of a stick-thin man seated in an oversized recliner, a long reed-like smoking stick protruding form his mouth, it spelled out in no uncertain terms, DICKMAN'S DEEP BURLEY BLEND. TWENTY POUNDS OF PIPE TOBACCO. OUR BEST MIXTURE. Eureka! I'd unearthed the world's largest bucket of mystery pipe weed.

At first, the grizzled old crow slouching behind that cha-chinging cash register seemed to have no earthly idea what it was I'd half rolled and half lugged up to his counter. We shared an awkward moment. The old geezer stared down at me slack-jawed, seeming to ponder whether I'd somehow unearthed the jaw bone of a woolly mammoth in and amongst his cereal boxes and cans of corned beef hash, and was now attempting to settle my tab with the confounding artifact included.

"Whatcha got there, Bub?" the crow asked toothlessly, sliding a wrinkled hand across his age-spotted brow. "Mind telling me what it says right there on the label? 'Cause ya see, these old peepers, they don't see like they usta."

"It says," and here I made an exaggerated point of quoting slowly and succinctly from the unequivocal label, just in case the old boy's ears were as decrepit as his eyes, "DICKMAN'S DEEP BURLEY BLEND. TWENTY POUNDS OF PIPE TOBACCO. OUR BEST MIXTURE."

"Well I'll be," the counterman positively cackled, "my great Uncle Toby usta hand mix that there pipe 'baccie right back yonder in the barn. A sizable number of good old boys would stop in regular as you please, just a wantin' to pick up a batch or two. Swore it was 'the best dern pipe 'baccie in the world.' For a goodly spell seemed Uncle Toby couldn't make enough of the galdern stuff. Then, just as sudden as that, for no reason any one of us could ever figger, they all just stopped comin' 'round. Uncle Toby, he's long gone now. So I suspect what you've got there, son, is the very last any of us will ever see of Dickman's Deep Burley Blend."

It's long been a theory of mine that every American has a suspicious consumer hidden somewhere in the inner recesses of their brain. My recessed shopper was now on full alert. He feared we'd fallen into the clutches of a master backwoods negotiator, one of those colorful characters that seem to inhabit every television sitcom under the sun. You know, the one who talks like a country bumpkin but thinks like a city fox. My inner suspicious consumer was telling me that this last bit of family treasure might just be about to cost us the clothes on our communal back and all the cash in our wallet to boot. But to his and my relief, it turned out the very last twenty pounds of Dickman's Deep Burley Blend in this world was neither too rare nor too dear to be purchased for a ridiculously paltry sum. A handshake and few dollars sealed the deal. Lashed to the rear fender of my sporty red Honda motorcycle with a spider's web of straining bungy cords, twenty pounds of Dickman's Deep Burley Blend was headed home to Jersey.

Now here's the thing. I'm a lifelong pipe smoker. Counting college to present day, I've probably burned my way through a small mountain of pipe tobacco. The wife, god bless her selfish little heart, nags that I've never met a tin of English tobacco I didn't have to jam into my pipe and smoke up. And if practice doesn't always make perfect, in most cases it at least renders us somewhat proficient. So without putting feathers in my cap that I have not earned, I don't believe I'd be telling a windy if I was to say I'm a bit of an old hand around the briar. The rituals, the things that must be done over and over until they become second nature in order to maximize the likelihood of enjoying a pipe, these I've mastered.

But there is one dark shameful secret I've carried around in my smoker's bosom all my pipe puffing years. Even though I smoke like a chimney, my pipes never acquire a cake. A dusting of carbon, a stain of tar, these I can muster. But when it comes to that nickel-thick badge of honor, the rock hard coating of carbon inside the bowl that literally separates pipemen from pipeboys, this has always eluded me.

But after smoking Dickman's Deep Burley Blend for the last month or so, I have this to report. First impression? Unbelievably tasty! I suspect it must be an aromatic of some sort. How else to explain why I crave it like dessert. It is that yummy. And I've identified another positive as well. Almost overnight—and in one or two cases literally overnight—my pipes have gone from having no cake at all to having the most manly of cakes. After just three or four bowls of Dickman's Deep Burley Blend, the usable tobacco chambers in my favorite pipes have been reduced by half.

And these are not soft cakes we're discussing here. Oh no. With Dickman's Deep Burley Blend there's no need to shake a spent pipe with thumb pressed to rim in order to artificially inseminate the bowl with ash. The almost instantaneous cakes that have presto appeared in all my pipes require no such chicanery. They simply appear. And when they do they defy the reamer. They laugh in the face of sharpened knives. If I might be allowed a single line of overheated rhetoric here, I'd say the blackened walls of carbonized armor that now guard the insides of all my pipes are the King Kong of cake!

The downside to this miracle-of-miracles is this. This wonder cake cannot be contained. I've always prided myself on how well I've cared for my pipes. Till recently there wasn't so much as a match burn or carbon shadow on the rim of a single one. Yet, with Dickman's Deep Burley Blend, in no time at all my pots and bulldogs and lumberman have literally boiled over. Cake a quarter inch thick has begun bubbling up and over the rims of all my pipes. In a few extreme cases it's even begun oozing down the outsides. The blackened tide of it cannot be contained. Like unstaunchable blood it hemorrhages everywhere.

Overnight I seem to have gone from being cake impotent to being a carbon stud of Homeric proportion. For better and for worse, thanks to Dickman's Deep Burley Blend, cake now adorns my precious pipes, inside and out, the same way fast-drying dipping fudge frosts a Dairy Queen softy cone. Impossible as it sounds, if my wondering eyes do not deceive me, this tar-like lava has even begun spreading to the racks where my pipes rest. Dare I suggest Dickman's mystery cake seems to possess magical powers of osmosis? With the virile contagion of a flesh eating disease it moves from host to host. Nothing and no one is safe from its odious flow.

As I'm sure you can imagine, after being cake deprived for so long, and now being the recipient of this unexpected bounty, my emotions are mixed. I feel, I suppose, like the middle-aged man must who's been told he'll never father children, who comes home one day only to have his wife inform him he's about to be the father of sextuplets.

And now there is this as well. Last night I pulled my most prized pipe, a GBD Virgin bent Rhodesian that my once almost human wife gave me as a wedding gift, down from its place of high honor, a special Scotty dog pipe rest atop the entertainment center. I stuffed it full of Dickman's Deep Burley Blend. After a good and thorough tamping I laid match to it. Long deep inhales got me nothing. Not a whiff of smoke passed my lips. The pipe is plugged. Creeping cake, I assume, has totally occluded its airway.

Not one to panic, I got out the trusty electric drill and a nice sharp five-sixteenth tungsten twist bit. Determined to restore order to my pipe smoking universe, in I went, whirring and grinding against an obstruction hard as stone that threatens to rob me of my peace of mind. Defying all reason and everything any of us have ever been told about tools by our fathers, even case-hardened tungsten whimpered and snapped when confronted by a thuggish plug of carbonized Dickman's Deep Burley Blend. Now, short of cutting off the shank of my favorite pipe and getting out the Vice-Grips, I don't believe the jagged shard of tungsten that remains impaled in my poor destroyed GBD will ever come out.

Sitting here tonight with pipe cake ooze hardening as we speak between my fingers, a small bubbling lake of it puddling atop my coffee table and dripping down onto my suede slippers, the internals of every pipe I own plugged irrevocably shut, I think I at last understand why those good old boys suddenly stopped coming around for their refills of the "best dern pipe 'baccie in the world."

Like a Dream

This old Barling had a severe oval shape. It looked like a flattened rubber pipe a forgetful fat man might have stuffed in his back pocket and then sat upon. Not a handsome pipe at all. True. Barling and Sons were silversmiths before they were pipemakers. And this little job did have a tarnished band 'round its shank to crow about. Give it that. But give it a slab of unreemed cake thick as an upholsterer's thumb and a straw's width of usable tobacco chamber as well. And while you're at it, two prominent cracks on opposing rims of the bowl, twin black rivers of destruction marking the open places where brittle wood lost its battle with expanding carbon.

"Why bid on such a pipe?" you ask. I had my reasons. For one, I'm not made of money. With less than a minute to go and that nerve jangling eBay counter clicking down the seconds, bidding on the piece had settled in on the cheapo side of fifty bucks. A mild financial beating, I'm thinking, especially for the cost—prohibitive pre-transition Barling I've always dreamed of owning. The other thing this particular baby had going for it was its hallmarked production date, 1919. I look for signs and patterns, messages in the seemingly ordinary. 1919 is the year both my mother and mother-in-law were born. A good omen, I thought.

And on top of that, I'm a bit of a history buff as well. And I recently read in an article by Barling collector/expert Tad Gage that back in the golden pre-transition days it was pretty much the norm for Barling pipemakers to be fashioning their handiwork from hundred-year-old wood. So, 1919 minus one hundred gets you to 1819. Admittedly, not a particularly historical date. But if you believe as I do, that almost every blessed thing under god's great sun is approximate, then the same 1919 minus one hundred just might get you where it got me . . . to 1812, a really big deal date in American history. Less than fifty bucks for a pipe fashioned from briar that was already a root in the ground back in the day when Yanks and Brits were lobbing cannonballs at each other on the high seas. How do you say "no" to a deal like that?

So anyway, I win the Barling and it arrives safely in the mail. That's always a crapshoot up here in the mountains I live in. Especially because out of spite over something I can no longer remember I refuse to put steps up to my porch and mailbox. And the postman, quite understandably, I think, counter-spites me by going out of his way to find obscure places all over my yard to leave my mail where it can't easily be found. But this pipe I find. I think it may have been under a bush behind the birdfeeder. And it's just as pictured, only half the size.

Now I've seen small pipes in my day. I once bought a Lindbergh commemorative pipe on eBay that was no bigger than a stick of gum. But this little Barling takes the cake. If General Tom Thumb was a pipe smoker (my jittery wife, who reads all my stuff before it goes out, always fretting I'll say something in print that will disgrace the family, tells me I should maybe mention who General Tom Thumb was. For those who know already, I apologize for insulting your intelligence. For those who don't, the dummies, the trivia challenged, General Tom Thumb was a famous, maybe the most famous, circus midget ever), this would for sure have been his pipe.

Now I know all about how the British, around the turn of the last century, supposedly smoked small pipes because the price of tobacco was so danged high. I can wrap my modern brain around that one. After all, the five-dollar per pound can of coffee I buy at my local A&P only weighs fourteen ounces. When prices go up big things tend to get little and nothing is ever again as it seems. The capitalist logic behind such insane market math is as old and easily understandable as greed. But could the cost of tobacco really ever have been high enough back in Victorian times to justify a pipe as small as this Barling? With a little help from aluminum foil, I've got hippie friends who smoke three hundred-dollar an ounce contraband in pipes bigger than this. But that's perhaps a yarn best left for another day's spinning.

So anyway, upon returning from my search and recovery mission to the birdbath with Barling in hand, I take it, cursing the postman every step of the way down, into the basement. There I get out the trusty Dremel, and like an insane dentist on a drilling spree to rid the world of decay, I manage to hollow out a cavity in the center of its double-cracked bowl wide enough to accept a few measly strands of tobacco. The miniscule oval thing I'm holding in my hand looks like a child's toy pipe. But I take a chance. I fire that sucker up. And I'll be a monkey's uncle if it doesn't smoke like a dream. "Yes," I say to myself, "this little Barling smokes like a dream." Those are my exact words.

Only thing is, every time I exhale into the stem, a habit I've gotten into as a means of modulating the rate of burn in my pipes kinda the way a blacksmith toys with his bellows, two tiny puffs of tobacco smoke pop out the side walls of my Barling. It's exactly as if that little oval bowl was a head and those twin cracks were two inverted ears on fire. I know. It sounds like I'm making all this up. But honest Injun, that's exactly what my cracked little Barling does. With a little provocation it spews tobacco smoke out its sides the way a sperm whale blows seawater out its blowhole. It's a hoot to see!

So I dial up Thom, this old friend who's living just outside Disneyland these days. We haven't seen each other in a dog's age. But among other things, Thom is a pipe-smoking madman. So when it comes to sharing tales of the Briar Brotherhood, he's tops on my list. So I tell him what I've just told you, about these horizontal blowholes in my Barling and how tobacco smoke shoots out of 'em like seawater from the top of a whale every time I exhale. And Thom tells me he's got this meerschaum with the figures of Watson and Holmes carved on its face. And he's wanted to tell me before but hasn't because he figured I'd rag on him for it, but he's drilled two tiny holes in Watson and Holmes mouths. And when he smokes that pipe he exhales down the stem and damned if those two detectives don't do a little exhaling themselves. Thom says he smokes that perforated meerschaum primarily when he's alone, because darned if he doesn't get the feeling those Baker Street boys are sharing a smoke with him. And here's the really spooky thing. Just like he was channeling me by parroting my exact thoughts, Thom says that meerschaum of his "smokes like a dream." Those were Thom's exact words so help me, "it smokes like a dream."

So my question here, my fellow pipe puffers, is this. Has anyone else out there tried this little modification? It's confession time. For once, don't let the cat get your tongue. This is no time for holding back. If we can muster a little honesty here, we might just be on the verge of a great pipe smoking breakthrough. So fess up, pipeaholics. Come clean. How many of you have taken a drill to the bowl of that lackluster pipe of yours, the sane ones simply tinkering in hopes of maybe making it smoke a little better, the less sane and more lonely among you doing a Frankenstein thing and make yourselves a pal?

And we're not talking stems here, people. They don't count. We're talking bowls! You, the lonely ones: in the privacy of your little smoking place have you ever sketched a comforting figure, maybe someone you enjoy referring to as "your smoking buddy," on the surface of your pipe and then drilled out the mouth in order to facilitate a little shared communication? So what if you have? And if you have, how has it all worked out for you? Do you, like my old pal Thom in Anaheim, find smoking that modified job to be "like a dream"? Let me hear from you on this. I really want to know.

No Reason I Can Fathom

A fellow pipe collector laments possessing an evil-smoking pipe carved in the likeness of French ex-president Charles de Gaulle. I wish I could say here that I found this revelation surprising. But as the owner of what I believe to be the world's largest collection of Charles de Gaulle-shaped smoking pipes, in truth, I found it to be anything but.

Of the almost two hundred Charles de Gaulle pipes I presently own, every stinking one smokes like a total rat. Why I collect the horrible things at all is a total mystery to me. Because like I say, it certainly isn't for any smoking satisfaction I get from them, because there isn't any. In fact, if forced to generalize (a small play on words right there, folks . . . "generalize" about "General" Charles de Gaulle, get it?), I'd have to say all Charles de Gaulle pipes are about as worthless in all regards as any smoking pipe can be.

My wonderful wife, god bless her little, selfish heart, is always screaming at the top of her surprisingly powerful lungs, "When are you gonna wise up, Bub, and sell all these disgustingly ugly Charles de Gaulle pipes?" And it behooves me to admit it, but I think the old battle-ax has a point. Because in addition to being lousy smokes, every pipe in my Charles de Gaulle collection is certainly nothing to look at either. Let's be frank (or Vera, Chuck or Dave—more stupid wordplay—sorry). Charles de Gaulle was, to put it mildly, an unattractive man. And just as no coin collector can ever say with a straight face that the Lincoln stamping on his pennies is handsome, no pipeman can ever crow about the gaunt puss on his Charles de Gaulle pipe bowl.

A confession. As possibly the world's greatest collector of such hideous pipes, it has long been my opinion that sculpted visages of extremely unattractive humans warp grain. And I further contend that such warped grain invariably diminishes taste. Anyway, that's how I see it. How else explain the fact that every Charles de Gaulle pipe in existence seems to be an evil smoker? Small differences in design seem to make no difference. I own some Charles de Gaulle pipes that draw freely and other are so constricted in their airways that the general seems have a cold. Most are engineered so the smoke chamber incorporates the deceased general's silly little military cap. One or two others, these being the very rarest and most collectable, have him carved bareheaded. Of necessity, these have their smoke chambers gouged deep down into the general's bony skull. And not a single one of these accursed pipes, capped or otherwise, smokes worth a tinker's gob.

So, to my disgruntled fellow collector, this is my considered advice to you. Perish all thought of improving the smokability of your Charles de Gaulle pipe. The intrinsic smoking flaws of such a tragically misguided smoking instrument are more than skin deep. A yacht with a square prow will never win the America's Cup. Wingless planes can never rise. And pipes carved in the likeness of General Charles de Gaulle of France will never smoke worth a hill of beans. So smoke the dreadful thing on July 14th if you must. But don't spend a single red cent attempting to improve it in any way. Such ultra-ugly pipes are beyond redemption by their very nature.

As a misguided collector of such novelty pipes, I can tell you with biblical certainty that briar mystically acquires the natures of the famous people it's carved to resemble. Does that seem far-fetched to you? Well, then I offer this further proof. I also happen to possess, again for no reason I can fathom, over four dozen Alex Trebek pipes. Most of them are highly collectable early production pieces sculpted back in the days when Alex was still sporting a mustache and glasses. And no matter what tobacco you load 'em up with, be it Erinmore Flake or Balkan Sobranie, they all smoke as if they were packed with musty old television cue cards. The celebrity curse is upon them all!

So take it from me, ralph in jersey, the world's greatest collector of worthless celebrity pipes. Save the money you're just itching to waste on that Charles de Gaulle upgrade. Put the cash in the cookie jar. And when you've got enough, snag yourself a Barling Ye Olde Wood on eBay.

Lethal and Loaded Weapon

Well, fellow pipe smokers, last night I got a glimpse of our future and it is not rosy. There's a gun being held to our heads, and the trigger of that lethal and loaded weapon is being squeezed by the shaky and nicotine-stained finger of our demonized brethren in smoke, the cigarette fiend. Allow me to explain.

My good buddy, Joe, is a retired phone company employee and cigarette junkie for life. But Joe is also one smart cookie. He knows those nasty butts are gonna do him in. But he doesn't care. That's because Joe's got what F. Scott Fitzgerald famously described as "the ability to hold two contradictory thoughts in the mind at once." He's smart and simultaneously comfortable doing a really dumbass thing. And he's not made of money either. The early pension deal he worked out with Ma Bell twenty years ago didn't include a cost of living provision. So today the astronomical cost of a carton of cigarettes is a train that left Joe's station without him.

Not one to be easily deterred, Joe does what junkies always do . . . whatever he must to service his addiction. For instance, in the interest of cost cutting, he's forsaken his lifelong cowboy companion the Marlboro Man for someone far less prestigious but far more affordable . . . Indians. Every pack of cigarettes Joe is smoking these days comes to him in the mail minus tax stamps with a portrait of one obscure Indian chief or another on the label. Now I'm not sure who these cigarette bootlegging "Indians" are. Do they actually have a recognizable tribal name and a legitimate reservation to call home? I doubt it. My entirely unfounded suspicion is they all speak Russian and inhabit a fringe enclave of New York City way out where subway lines meet up with sandy beaches. But wherever they live and whatever language they speak, for sure these tobacco-dealing Redskins are doing a land office business with my friend Joe.

Then, the word from Joe was that the U.S. Post Office was balking at shipping tobacco-related contraband. And so he began rolling his own smokes. Joe became a regular at a local "smoke shop" that doesn't sell pipes or cigars. What they do sell to the exclusion of all else are bulk bags of tobacco and machines for jamming it into pre-formed, empty cigarette paper. You can purchase these tube-shaped vessels with and without filters, in most every color of the rainbow from pink to black. And the machines designed to fill them are something to see. The most elaborate come complete with stainless steel sorting trays, troughs for gathering pre-measured loads of tobacco and fun-to-operate levers for ramming it home. "A pack a butts in less den ten minutes at about half a da cost" is the way the bent-nosed "tobacconist" in charge explained the whole scenario to me.

And what does all this have to do with pipe smoking, you ask? Just this. That bulk tobacco being sold in large bags to supply all those nifty machines being sold in "tobacco shops" without pipes and cigars looks and smells very much like pipe tobacco. In fact, it looks and smells so much like our precious pipe weed that the distinction between the two is, well, for all intents and purposes, indistinguishable. If marketed as cigarette tobacco it is subject to an onerous tax. If marketed as pipe tobacco—forgetting for the moment where it is actually intended to land up—it is not. Now, fellow pipe smokers, do you begin to see where all this runaway tobacco subterfuge is headed and who's about to get mowed down?

Because dollars to donuts the Smoke Nazis in Washington are not oblivious to what's going on. But what's to be done? To anyone other than a tobacco blender or smoking aficionado, we're dealing with two near identical products, one capable of raising vast revenues for the greedy Great White Father in Washington, the other not so. So smart money and common sense tell me this Gordian Knot is about to get cut in a way that's gonna cause lots of blood and pain in the pipe community.

And that's not the end of my cautionary tale. The "Indians" are apparently not taking all that postal embargo nonsense lying down. Last night the wife and I attended old friend Joe's annual Christmas gala. He tells me he no longer smokes cigarettes. To prove his point, he pulls out a pack of what looks exactly like cigarettes, only on the label, directly atop the picture of a generic Indian chieftain, it clearly states the package contains TWENTY SMALL CIGARS.

But these "cigars" look exactly like cigarettes—same circumference, same paper, right on down to their long, slender filter. And old friend Joe is telling me how these "cigars" are milder than the mildest cigarette and don't make "tons of smoke like other smelly cigars do." And you know something? They don't. And the reason they don't is because if the little smokes Joe is puffing on and inhaling are cigars, then pigs can fly and Rick Perry is gonna be the next President of the United States. These little babies are wolves in sheep's clothing, cigarettes in brown paper. And, of course, they cost half as much as cigarettes because, you guessed it . . . no troublesome stamps inside the cellophane and no onerous tax! And to complete Joe's happy trifecta, they're coming to his door once again courtesy of the good old U.S. Mail.

Now I say again, this sort of tax-evading tomfoolery won't go on much longer. I can't tell you Uncle Sam is no fool—but I will tell you he's a fool who loves his money. And I don't believe he's got the patience or the expertise to decide what's pipe tobacco and what's bulk cigarette tobacco, and what's a "small cigar" and what's a thin, brown cigarette. Am I alone here, people, in thinking all these Indian shenanigans are gonna end ugly for us pipe smokers? If you ask me, in the end the baby is going out with the bath water. Mr. Taxman is gonna call this game in favor of the home team, his team, the Great White Father's team, and just say all tobacco, even my very own indispensable Compton's Macedonian Blend, is subject to a single universal onerous tax. And when it goes down that way and all our precious two-ounce tins of Early Morning Blend and Red Rapparie arrive wreathed in a rainbow of multi-colored tax stamps, take it from ralph in jersey. We're all gonna have the penny-pinching cigarette smokers and their cronies in crime, the Russian "Indians," to blame for the mess.

Troubles in Toyland

Am I alone here, people, in thinking something strange is happening in the eBay estate pipe market? Overnight the price of old pipes seems to have shot up through the roof. A year ago I picked up a GBD Century bent Rhodesian in really nice condition in a tame little auction for forty bucks. Right now, as we speak, the same shaped pipe but in the bush league Digby line with the far less desirable Rockroot finish is being bid up over a hundred-and-a-half.

It's the same craziness with the Italian stuff. Not long ago I added a nice old Ascorti rusticated billiard with a smooth rim to my collection. Price? The mind is shot so I can't be exact, but for sure it was less than fifty bucks. Today its kissing cousin, an almost identical Caminetto of similar vintage, is being offered BUY IT NOW for again, over a hundred-and-a-half. And another very distinctive twin signature Caminetto, this one a smooth finished stack billiard I bid on and lost a few months back at around one-sixty, is back on the market, this time as a BUY IT NOW for over three-hundred.

Now this. Two Charatan Supremes, both really nice pipes but nothing one-of-a-kind or really ancient, are being offered from the same seller. A year ago they were both hundred-dollar pieces. Today, one sold for an astounding two-thirty, the other for three-fifty. What gives?

The pattern I see here doesn't particularly surprise me. The price of everything from chewing gum to bailing wire has gone haywire. So you'd expect the cost of used pipes to keep pace. But what does puzzle me is how suddenly every available piece of used briar has skyrocketed almost overnight. It's as though a billion free-spending Chinese decided to jump into our used pipe market with their inflation-provoking little feet flailing. Or maybe it's game-on between Bill Gates and Donald Trump in a billionaire's death match to see who can buy up every last stick of old briar in the world.

I'm an optimist by nature. I'm hoping this spike in used pipe prices I think I'm noticing is just an aberration, a troubling visitation brought on by a Dickensonian bit of undigested beef. Or have others of you been having the same nasty dream of late?

Apropos of Nothing

I've suggested somewhere that investing major money in the purchase of an "art pipe" was to convince oneself in advance that the pipe in question could only be a great smoker. Perhaps not surprisingly, as a consequence, one purveyor of such ultra-high end merchandise rose to his own defense. In a published reply he contends, "folks who regularly buy high grades to smoke . . . do not 'fool themselves'." The single quotation marks, I think, were unfairly meant to be attributable to me.

But I love pipes. I love pipe smokers. I love grizzled men who jam drugstore pipes in their craw as they operate forklifts and service elevators, and I love their more materially fortunate brethren who inhabit spacious studies and adorn their lips with patent Dunhills. So why—if I indeed had—would I accuse any brother or sister of the briar of something as base as "fooling themselves"? Well, the answer as it turns out is I hadn't. Nowhere had I used the words "fool themselves" to describe anyone.

The exact words I'd used were "to convince oneself in advance." I chose these words, my words, carefully, hoping to describe a malady perhaps closely related to out-and-out self-deception, but of a slightly different, less lethal strain. "Fooling," when the act is applied to oneself, conjures for me unflattering images of weakness and sleazy deception. "Convincing oneself in advance," on the other hand, is something men of high character and superior intellect do every day as a matter of course. Doctors of human nature instruct us that in matters both grave and frivolous, the full gamut of decision-making spanning everything from who we love and who we vote for to what cereal box we pull down from that deviously designed supermarket shelf, the science of comprehending human choice is rooted not so much in what we observe as in how we are predisposed to see it.

Predisposition shapes perception. Sadly, it's just how we humans tick. And even the most magisterially aloof pipe smoker garbed in double-breasted valor and swaddled in Corinthian leather upholstery is not immune to the immutable laws of science. I think we might agree here that to accuse a fellow puffer of being swept into a storm drain of scientifically verifiable behavior is a far cry from composing an obituary having him drowned outright in a flood of his own folly. So although my defense hinges on both a careful and accurate reading of my words, I believe I'll stand by them.

Which apropos of nothing brings me to this. By way of explaining what actually does happen to "art pipes" that are purchased and turn out to be disappointing smokers, it is pointed out in the article rebutting mine that they are "quickly resold and the proceeds used to fund another." This seems feasible. But if true, it leads my mind down a path of inquiry that runs uncomfortably near the third rail of all used pipe transactions: truth in advertising.

Hardly an estate pipe is posted on eBay in which the seller does not go to painful lengths to describe the pipe in exacting detail, both in words and pictures. But who among us recalls ever having read a word in a single solicitation pertaining to any pipe's smokability? I would contend that to the average used pipe buyer nothing is more important to the purchase of any pipe than how it smokes. And yet, as a community, it would seem we've all agreed by silent assent that any and all reference to this all important marker of value be deleted from our transactions. Sellers don't make mention of it when listing a pipe's assets and flaws, and stranger still, buyers don't make mention of it when invited to ask questions. What's that about?

I've got some thoughts on the subject. Firstly, I find it suspicious that almost everyone on eBay selling a used pipe seems to be a non-smoker. Ever notice how many ads include the disclaimer "we don't know much about pipes so be sure to take a good look and ask lots of questions . . . which we'll answer if we can." How can so many smoking pipes be mysteriously falling into the hands of people who know nothing about them? If the objects being sold were guns or lie detectors or suitcase nukes, would we all accept such ridiculous disclaimers on faith? I think not.

It is my suspicion that many sellers of used pipes know far more than they're telling. And what about all the pipes being sold for friends and deceased grandfathers and yes, by third-party agents? Does it ever occur to anyone other than me that the only thing all these sellers have in common is a ready-made excuse to know nothing about how the pipe in question smokes? Sure, we could always ask grandpa how his pipe smoked. After all, the seller has just offered to be helpful in the extreme. But then again, he's also just told us grandpa is dead. Check and mate! Matter closed.

Let's be honest. Nobody sells their favorite pipe while there's still breath in their warm body. As pipe junkies we spend our entire lives combing world markets in sleepless search of the "perfect smoke." Why, in the name of common sense then, would any nincompoop among us ever sell one? So as buyers we can't and don't expect the moon. And anyway, if anyone ever did sell the best they had, they'd likely say, "hey, this baby is my all-time favorite and it smokes like a dream." But nobody ever says things like that about their pipe. Why? Perhaps because that might open a can of worms and then they'd have to 'fess up about the bad ones too. Let's face it. How many pipes can any single seller market as his "all-time favorite" before the story starts wearing thin?

So the subject of smokability goes untouched, even by the most scrupulously honest sellers in our midst. I even have a theory as to how they justify it to themselves. It's that myth rampant among us that a pipe that smokes poorly for one pipeman just might smoke like a dream for another. Like Simon and Garfunkle sang it in the Seventies, "one man's ceiling is another man's floor." And when it comes to apartment units jumbled one atop another, that just makes good architectural sense. But when it comes to an evil-smoking pipe, it basically makes no sense whatsoever. But we pipemen perpetuate it like it was gospel. It enables us with clear conscience to gather up the gurglers and the burners of flesh and pass them along in the sure and fervent hope that they'll be reborn as favorites in someone else's fireproof hands.

Finally, before leaving you all to do your own pipeman thinking, it's occurred to me somewhere along the line here that I've not been completely forthcoming. I believe I inferred previously that I could not recall a single eBay seller who'd addressed the issue of pipe smokability. I now realize this is not quite true. One startling exception has come to mind, and although I've been thinking for some paragraphs now I'd find a clever writerly (no such word . . . no need to check) way to weave this revelation into my tale, this piece is all but over and I've still got this to say. I believe it may have been Marty Pulvers on his most excellent and most funny website who almost broke the code of pipe omerta. In discussing a little Peterson Dublin with a P-stem, I believe it was Marty who said something along these lines: "Due to a severe case of stem restriction, a condition common to many Petersons and this one in particular, I suggest this little Dublin be purchased as an item of visual admiration as opposed to a smoking instrument." That's as close as I've seen any pipe seller get to grabbing our crackling third rail. If it was indeed you who said it, Marty, thanks!

Avoiding Pots Like the Plague

1. Gonna buy a pipe? Make it a good one. Will it be guaranteed to smoke any better than a cheapo drugstore job? Hell no! But for better or worse, we become forever associated with the objects we possess. Take James Dean. The guy is an undeniable legend. He died head-oning his Porsche 550 Spyder into a two-tone Ford coupe driven by a man with the unlikeliest of names . . . Donald Turnupseed. Now ponder this. How different might we all feel about James Dean if it he'd smashed himself to bits in a Nash Rambler on that sleepy Salinas highway? Would he even be a legend? So whatever else you do, remember this. Brand association is important. Don't let anyone tell you otherwise. Buy yourself a pipe with a name on it that others can recognize and respect. At the very least it will do wonders for your self-image, and some day it just might jazz up your obituary.

2. Pipe pundits will tell you there are three basic types of pipe smoking tobacco: English, Virginia and aromatic. Aromatics suck. So really there are only two legitimate choices when choosing pipe tobacco. Here, I think, we can all take a lesson from the movie Mogambo. You know, the one with Clark Gable playing the randy big-game hunter who's gotta make a choice between bedding Grace Kelly or Ava Gardner. Which lady is hotter? Which one is gonna make buwana happier in the sack? Who cares? The way I

look at it, the whole point of that stupid jungle movie is this: sometimes, faced with two really good choices, even an imbecile can't mess up. English/Ava? Virginia/Grace? You choose. You really can't mess up.

3. When packing a pipe, there must be ten thousand different methods you can try. I practice the ralph in jersey tried-and-true gravity method. I call it that because unlike some other methods, you don't have to turn your pipe upside down or sideways. No need to be ambidextrous with the ralph in jersey method. All you need is a wild imagination and a willingness to pretend you're piloting a B-52. Ready for action? Okay, bombs away! Drop enough loose tobacco into your pipe to fill it to the top. Now, with a tamper, and again, make it the fanciest you can afford just in case it too gets mentioned in your obituary, press down just hard enough and far enough so that the tobacco compresses into a level disc. Not one silly millimeter more do you wanna go. I enjoy thinking of this part as "bouncing on a mattress," 'cause if you're doing it just right and have the capacity to hold two unrelated but strangely supportive images in your mind simultaneously, that's about what it's gonna feel like. Usually, with me, if I've loose-packed the pipe to the rim and jumped on that mattress just till it feels "springy," I now find myself looking down the bore of a bowl that's about two-thirds to three-quarters full of ready to light yummy pipe tobacco.

4. Now there are those in our midst who would have you repeat this process over and over till the bowl is full. But ralph in jersey says "why bother?" Let's face it. We live in a testosterone-driven age where everything that's bigger and fuller is assumed for no good reason to be better. But it just ain't so. I mean, why must everyone's dog suddenly be pony-sized? Am I the only person in the world who misses seeing an occasional beagle or cocker spaniel peeing on a

hydrant, or for that matter, a pipe half full? An average-sized pipe filled to three-quarters capacity and smoked properly will last you all through the Sunday morning news shows. Or, if you're a sports junkie, maybe into the seventh inning of a typical Red Sox-Yankees baseball marathon. Remember, Alf Dunhill, the Abe Lincoln of pipe smoking, said "Sip, don't gulp." Follow the great man's advice (Dunhill's, not mine) and you'll see I'm right. And there's this too. If your pipe is only three-quarters full when you go at it with one of those big old wooden kitchen matches, you're far less likely to scorch the rim and burn the couch. Especially if you're like me and you're knocking back single malts with one hand and puffing away like a fiend with the other.

5. Now, if you draw on that stem of yours and are rewarded with a wheezeless puff of fresh air that moves effortlessly through loose-packed tobacco the way a nasty rumor runs rampant through a political convention, then, and only then, are you ready for that stick match. Now the first match is the "charring light." It raises and obliterates that springy disc of flat tobacco you worked so tirelessly to create. But don't despair. Simply re-tamp, again, always with thoughts of a springy mattress in your mind, and fire 'er up again. And this time, really over-light that baby. Even though breathing fire is nobody's idea of a good time, really pull that flame down into the crown of your tobacco until it looks like a hill of fire. Hey, you can always cool things down with a little slow puffing once you're well and truly under way. But if you fail to attain total blastoff from the get-go, your pipe smoking experience will always be sketchy at best.

6. By "sketchy," I mean this. Not all pipes light evenly. From experience I can tell you that pipes with good cake seem to pull that glowing crown of fire outward toward the edges of the bowl. It's almost like that carbon liner attracts fire. I can

also tell you pipes with narrower tobacco chambers, billiards and bulldogs and rhodesians, are easier to ignite fully than the wider bowled guys like the pots. Personally, I avoid pots like the plague for this very reason. For, you see, my imagination is, well, for lack of a kinder word let's just call it athletic. 'Cause while I'm smoking I'm always fantasizing about what path that fire might be taking through all those jangled up tobacco shards. The journey, as I envision it, is never an easy or an even one. One moment my fevered mind might have the burn tunneling down the center and then up the sides—this without any factual confirmation that a smoldering burn such as the one in smoking pipes is even physically capable of burning upward through tobacco—and in the next having it moving laterally. I even have an entirely unsubstantiated theory that such rogue lateral burns are the cause of nine out of ten pipe burn-outs. And because I am afflicted with such silly thoughts, I avoid pots like the plague and approach all pipe lightings in deadly earnest.

7. I read recently—I think it may have been right here in the Collector—that a pipe can be smoked up to four times on one filling. After almost a half-century of uninformed puffing, this came as a thunderbolt revelation to me. Yes, like most pipemen, I think nothing of lighting and re-lighting a bowl of tobacco until, in my mind, it seems reasonable to think the tobacco has been totally consumed. Well, all right, not even consumed. Just almost consumed. For always, with me, there is that bit of wet dottle at the bottom, the icky plug that must be picked out after all the blessed white ash has been tapped away. Dottle, the pipeman's brown badge of shame. But always, in my mind, with repeated re-lighting the unsmokable goop is reached and the bowl is considered finished. And then came this revelation about pipe tobacco rebirth. So now, in my home, full pipes once considered finished sit overnight in their

Scotty dog and Bengal tiger holders, waiting to be re-fired and re-enjoyed in the morning. And I say "re-enjoyed" because miracle-of-miracles, often the second and third go-rounds are better than the first. I attribute this, again, independent of any corroborating evidence, to the fact that I've always enjoyed my pipe tobacco extra dry. Give me a sealed tin of fresh tobaccie. First thing I'll do is bash open the lid with the nearest blunt instrument and expose the contents to blasts of drying air. And that's no easy trick when you inhabit the swampy climes of mosquito-infested New Jersey. Nine days out of ten, in the Garden State an open tin of tobacco is more likely to go soupy than crispy. The soggy gas we call "air" here in Jersey really is that wet! Hair dryers, baking ovens, blowtorches, even pouches lashed tight to the exhaust pipes of running cars . . . I've tried every trick there is to put some crackle in my pipe tobacco. And still it seems I'm continually doomed to disappointment. So not surprisingly, the groundless theory of tobacco reconstitution I've devised states that even ultra-dry tobacco, once subjected to the heat of initial firing, dries out even further. It gets toasted, I enjoy thinking, in a furnace of its own making. How's that for an unsubstantiated image?!

8. So there they are, all my undisciplined thoughts on the mundane, technical aspects of our hobby. Whether a single word of what I've said here is factual I leave to each of you to decide. If any or all of it is contrary to your experience, go with what you think you know. If you do all that I suggest, I'm not going to sit here and tell you that you can't go wrong. You can and probably will. But hey, I contend that making the same stupid mistakes over and over again is a big part of the fun of pipe smoking.

"I mean, why must everyone's dog suddenly be pony-sized? Am I the only person in the world who misses seeing an occasional beagle . . ."

Tad and Joe Under Fire

If you love pipes and read pipe magazines (and if you don't, what in god's name are you doing reading me here?), then you are familiar with Tad Gage and Joe Harb's good works in Pipes and Tobaccos Magazine. Tad and Joe are those lucky dogs who get paid (one assumes such guys get paid, right?) to smoke all those yummy pipe tobaccos and render their expert opinions (again, one assumes anyone who has been previously assumed to be getting paid to do a task anyone else in their right mind would do for free must have an opinion that is expert, right?) on their relative merits. They call their column Trial By Fire. It's a hoot.

If Tad and Joe can be believed (and because they are quite obviously pipe smokers, I believe they can), the simplest of tobacco blends can undergo more flavor transformations than Carter's got liver pills (ask the old puffer in your family to explain that reference). Yup, with Tad and Joe a bowl of straight Virginia might kick off with caramelized pecan overtones, blossom mid-burn into something unexpectedly floral, only to suffer a smoldering Raisinette-like death at the base. To be honest, sometimes sharing a bowl in print with Tad and Joe can feel a little like being dragged open-mouthed over a fruit stand and down a confectioner's counter. Sometimes all the flavor variations seem beyond me.

And I blame myself for not being able to find that hint of anisette in my latikia or tincture of burnt orange in the burley. I think with me it's an occupational thing. I say this because when I was a kid I distinctly remember being able to smell like that. I'd be lying on the back floor of my father's 1950 Ford (I would have been stretched out on the more comfortable back seat but my older and stronger sister was already there), my head pillowed against the anvil-hard ledge that protruded from beneath those old door frames, my backside and inner thighs raised in a perfectly formed "V" over the carpeted hump of the drive-axle. And when that old jalopy got itself up on the George Washington Bridge, Manhattan shimmering like diamonds on velvet in the rearview, the costume jewelry of Fort Lee dead ahead, the fragrance of trees and bushes and maybe a million unseen midnight lawns would come wafting up in one great, rolling mass to greet me. Jersey air!

I tell you, you never forget that sort of smell performance!

Today, a thousand dusty rip-outs and a billion linear board feet of framing timber cut to fit later, I can no longer smell my own name (I know, that technically makes no sense, but it was fun to write and then to read, and I think you catch my drift). My sinuses are a mining disaster, airways permanently, occupationally collapsed at the timbers. And you know what they say. When you can't smell you can't taste. So when I tell you I recognize the difference between a hamburger and a hotdog by remembering that the hotdog is the one that snaps when I bite down, you can take that to the bank. And when I tell you that wordy tobacco reviews like Tad and Joe's are but oil paintings set before the blind when presented to olfactorilly (no, there is no such word, you need not check) challenged men like myself, you can safely deposit that as well.

I smoke English tobacco. Began in the Sixties with Balkan Sobranie in the white tin. It was love at first puff. And I never looked back until it didn't do me any good to keep looking forward. Because all of a sudden all my beloved white Balkan Sobranie tins disappeared. And with them went that strange cover art. Goodbye boarded-up gypsy wagons. Adios jagged hills and gaunt women in flowing dresses smoking long pipes atop a rockslide as though it were an English tea party (say, who were those strange, cartoonish people on those Sobranie labels suppose to be anyhow, Balkans?).

My beloved Sobranie is gone. Good-bye yummy Yenedje! Like a mourner at a funeral, I've had to reconcile myself to the fact that when some things are gone, they are gone forever. The Good Old Days are not coming back. So I'm toughing it out. Of late I've been spending upwards of forty bucks, very nearly the same ransom I've grown accustom to paying on eBay for most of my used (excuse my misuse of the vernacular. what I meant to say, of course, was "estate") pipes, for "collector tins" of English tobacco. Mostly Dunhill My Mixture 965, or sometimes, for a change, it might be the more werewolfian (again, no such word exists) Nightcap if the perique moon is full and I've gone all furry.

But it's always English blends with me. Everything must always be disturbingly similar in order to suit my taste. And amongst things that are similar, everything tastes pretty much the same to me. Now I'm not gonna tell you that if I fill my bowl with straight burley or Escudo or Navy Flake or even, saints preserve us, Erinmore, I'm not gonna notice a difference. But what I will tell you is that difference makes no difference, because I'm not gonna fill my bowl with any of those squirrelly tobaccies. Because like I've already mentioned several times, with me it's English blend or it's nothing at all (again, ask the old puffer in the house to explain the commercial reference). And the differences between one English and another for me, assuming those English blends are closely related, as they must be if

I'm going to put them in my pipe, make no difference either because to me they all taste swell.

"Swell." Now how's that for a non-Tad and Joe one-word tobacco review . . . "that English tobacco (remember, if asked, I could only do reviews of English blends 'cause like I've already said, I won't put any other in my bowl) was swell." And what, you ask, does "swell" taste like? You think I'd know at least that much, right? I mean, after what, ten thousand bowls of the same taste over the course of damn near a full lifetime, you'd think the answer to that question would be a no-brainer. But it isn't. And I'll tell you why. Upon reflection I've come up with this (I'm learning at the same time you are here—a sign, I think, that the writing process is working) . . . some tastes are divisible only by themselves. From tonight onward I believe I will refer to them as "prime tastes." You can do likewise if you'd like.

If you don't smoke a pipe, to come to grips with such a concept you might want to think of water. What if someone asked you right now, "what does pure, cold spring water taste like?" Simple, right? Anybody'd recognize that familiar taste in a heartbeat. But it isn't. Because pure water only tastes like one thing on earth . . . itself, water. You damn well know it when it's in your mouth. But just try describing it to someone else without using that word, "water." If that word is unspoken you haven't said damn near enough, and once it's said there really shouldn't be anything further to add. That, to me, is a "prime taste."

Well, the taste of my English tobacco is, I believe, such a prime taste. Why? Because it tastes like nothing other than itself. And that taste is too complex to be captured in kitchen-flavored "sister tastes" like chocolate and butterscotch and bitterroot. Okay, it might begin as something as mundane. But my tobacco, like the nebulous smoke clouds it produces, has the magical capacity to grow into a tornado of tastes, swooping up everything in proximity to it. Before we are done together, the taste of my English tobacco might include dinner and the scotch before and after, the butter-soft leather arm of my battered and oft patched smoking chair, the softer still whisper of my wife asking when I'll be ready for coffee, and yeah, that old familiar messenger nicotine running around my brain heralding the fact that tonight again life is good and my crazy little world is safe. How's that for a complex "prime taste"?

Well, it's not likely I'd get around to blathering any such stuff, even if some tobacco magazine editor was reckless enough to give me a guest shot at Tad and Joe's gig. I'd probably just settle for some nice comfortable one-liner like "that English tobacco was swell." Figure I might get away with one or two reviews like that. A small cadre of readers out there suffering a mild dose of, well, let's just call it putting too fine an edge on things that sometimes don't call for such fine edging, might even find my one-line reviews a refreshing change of pace . . . at first. "That English tobacco smells swell!" "That English tobacco tastes swell." "That English tobacco is swell."

But even I have to agree that after several issues and a dozen or so such redundant reviews in which the only mixtures reviewed are remarkably similar English affairs and the only word used to either praise or deride any of them is "swell," well, even I have to admit that after a time such parrot jabber might begin to chafe. I suspect that's the reason lucky dogs like Tad and Joe will always have the swell job they do.

Little Slap On the Bottom

Pipe smokers, at least all the ones I've read in the pages of the Pipe Collector, pride themselves on the inclusiveness of our hobby. They see the Brotherhood of the Briar spanning the gap between collectors of priceless Bo Nordh freehands as works of art to be put unsmoked behind locked glass on the one hand, to hoarders of shoeboxes of abused and oversmoked Kaywoodies and Dr. Grabow's on the other. Within the pages of the Pipe Collector I've just finished reading a transcription of a speech given by Rick Newcombe at the 2009 West Coast Pipe Show, titled TELL ME WHAT YOU LIKE. Unless I misinterpret, what Rick has given us here is a codified ode to friendship within our smoky fraternity. And I wholeheartedly agree with every word he's written. If I might paraphrase, Rick's central thrust seems to be this . . . I may not collect what you collect, but show me what you've got and I will be glad to see it, because, by god, we are both brothers in the briar.

Who could reasonably take issue with such a call for egality within the brotherhood? But I wish to say two things to those good souls who publish the Pipe Collector. First, you're doing one hell of fine job. The Pipe Collector is the best damn forum dealing with our hobby, period. And now, having patted your head with my right hand, I will give you a little slap on the bottom with my left. Editors of the Pipe Collector, our hobby is even broader than you suspect. Some very strange people, myself included, smoke pipes. So an occasional transmission from the fringe might be sorely welcomed in your pages.

Your regular contributors are without doubt the life's blood of this publication. They are all wonderfully informative. Many are side-splittingly humorous. All give unselfishly of their time and resources for the betterment and pleasure of us all. For better and worse, they are the vanguard of modern pipe collecting in the U.S. And yet, all their voices can seem at times to be coming from one small spectrum of the hobby . . . from the private pre-show suites most of us never enter, from a rarified strata of privilege exemplified by patent Dunhill magnums and collector pieces that dwarf the purse of the working man. I know. This is the meat and potatoes of our hobby. Without those suites and without this group's financial wherewithal, all the aspiring pipe artists of the New Golden Age of Pipe Smoking would starve for sure. I know I can't afford to feed them.

But having said all that, Mr. Newcombe has challenged the rest of us, the thirty-dollar estate pipe set, to speak out. If we do, he assures us he will listen. He smokes a pipe. In my world this makes him a good man till I know otherwise. I take his word as gospel. So let the gauntlet be thrown down. Speak up, all my strange-thinking oddball brothers in the briar. But know this. If we do not write, if we do not contribute odd little tales of our own small failures and triumphs, we fail ourselves. And if we do write and our voices do not find their way in some small way into this otherwise fine publication, then the Pipe Collector has failed us.

The Silence
of the Pipes

The pipes are worried. Like me, they're old and set in their ways. To a non-man there's not a spring chicken in the bunch. Counting prenatal growing time hunkered down in inhospitable Mediterranean soil, misspent adolescences spent drying inside someone's musty burlap sack and time tacked on in the workaday world as much beloved smoking instruments, the wood in most of my pipes is easily over a hundred years old. And you know what they say about age . . . that with it hopefully comes a modicum of wisdom. So from the brightest of my pipes, a plateau-topped Danish freehand I'm convinced would scribble calculus on a blackboard if given hands and a piece of chalk, to the dummy of the bunch, a P-lipped bent Peterson who barely knows his button from his bowl, they can all see I'm not the man I was. And it doesn't take a Mensa pipe to figure out that if something happens to me, things around here are gonna get dire for briar. Reassuringly predictable days spent lounging in comfortable racks as members of one big happy smoking family will be kaput.

I know the concept of pipes as family must seem strange to some of you. Why, I read in this very newsletter about one take-no-prisoners pipe collector who gives new briar ten smokes to get it right before shipping it off. Other shameless stalwarts of our hobby nonchalantly confess to shifts in interest that overnight obliterate whole collections. In a pipe family such wanton acts of pipe violence are incomprehensible.

Why, I could no more liquidate a pipe from my collection for substandard performance than dream of putting up one of my biological children for adoption over a poor report card.

Nobody is perfect in this house, least of all me. Perfection is not even a standard we aspire to. Effort and improvement, these are the lower hurdles we strive to clear every day. Sure, sure, if by some miracle a life-transforming perfect smoke should happily present itself, we know how to celebrate around here. But we throw deliriously merry parties for an adequate smoke from a pipe that last month might have been terrible as well. For you see, in this home we subscribe to a theology of pipe puffing which allows for the redemption of less than perfect briar. So around here even grossly deficient pipes are not photographed like common criminals and subjected to the public humiliation of penny ante eBay auctions.

What my pipes do for me in return for this loyalty is a bit harder to explain. I'll be sixty-five this April. The world I live in has grown too strange and rapid-fire for me. These days, if beaten ferociously about the head or held underwater till almost drowned or just simply asked politely, I'll confess to feeling like a retarded alien visitor on my children's planet. If asked to describe myself as a car, I'd have to say I'm a 1957 Chevy wagon, a road tank with a chrome bullet for a steering wheel and a rear seat custom made for propagating the species, rusting away ingloriously on somebody else's 21st Century driveway. I'm slow. I'm out of sync. My wife, that master of the subtle and emasculating dig, refers to me whenever the hurtful opportunity arises as "a man of few words."

And it behooves me to admit it, but the old battle-ax is not entirely wrong. Loquacious I am not. I suppose it's partially because I've allowed my mind to be led into a box canyon of thought that goes something like this. It seems to me that for any sort of meaningful communication to take place, the profound thing being discussed must be pre-understood on some shared fundamental level by both parties attempting to do the communicating. But if such pre-understanding exists, then the communication is unnecessary. And if it is lacking, well, then real meaningful communication is impossible. As a logical corollary to that train of thought, I can't help noticing that ninety-nine percent of what passes for day-to-day chatter does not matter.

Or maybe the truth is harsher still. Perhaps I'm simply a strange man who's been saying strange things for so long to the same long-suffering audience that there's nobody still here listening. On pitch-black mornings when I've gotten up to take a piss because my prostate is shot and my mind decides everything is just too dire for getting back to sleep, I find it strangely comforting thinking of myself as a lousy entertainer who long ago sent his audience stampeding to the exits, but out of some psychotic compulsion goes right on with the act. Yes, maybe that's it. But for sure, my communication skills have been seriously impaired. And crazy as this sounds, my pipes understand this. They accept me on my own mute terms. Daily they ask nothing more of me than a pinch of tobacco properly tamped, the fire of a match and my undivided attention for the short time it takes to lay ash to a bowl of tobacco.

It's not a lot to ask. In return my pipes perch warm and balanced beneath my nose, content in their pipish way to be engulfed in clouds of thick gray smoke and the deafening quiet of an ugly old man gone quite strange. They do not jabber. If they have something important to say, they are wise enough to not say it. Like Eastern mystics they teach by example. Foolish, unobservant people mistake this silence of the pipes for stupidity. As for me, I've got another theory. I'm convinced my wise little pipes are intently listening to every single word I do not speak but only think.

Moonday

The first time I encountered Karl the Tobacconist, he was fully engaged in a violent one-sided verbal altercation with a ruddy-faced customer easily twice his size. This menacing mountain of a man had the entire upper half of his massive frame suspended crane-like across a glass pipe case, his hands two knotted fists, his forehead a purple symphony of pulsating veins and arteries.

To the little man standing more beneath than before him, this giant shouted, "For the last time, Karl, I'm telling you. You're gonna have my pipes back to me by Friday. Friday, do you understand? Or so help me, Karl, I'm comin' back in here and poke your eyeballs out with one of these shiny pipes of yours. Do I make myself clear, Karl? This Friday is judgment day for you."

It's been forty years since that day, and I honestly can't recall whether my initial instinct was to intervene, cower, or more cowardly still, run like a madman. Moments before I'd been carefree and footloose as a fat mouse at a grain convention. I was outside. It was sunny. Nobody was shouting. The topic of bodily harm was a zillion miles from my mind. And then there'd been that inexplicable urge to go inside and have a confidential little chat with the proprietor of this wonderful smelling tobacco shop about my nasty cigarette addiction.

So I stepped inside the door of that little smoke shop, and what I do recall vividly is how unflappable that little tobacconist with his squirrelly metal-framed glasses, rumpled dress shirt and bow tie seemed. The more Angry Customer Man gritted and growled, the more Karl the Tobacconist smiled. And not just any smile, mind you. His was a smile so inappropriately detached from all that was going on as to make him seem a perfect simpleton. Did Karl the Tobacconist understand a single word Angry Customer Man was saying? Was he even casually interested in his own personal safety? If so, nothing in his serene demeanor hinted at those facts.

In a complete inversion of what might have been expected, the more Angry Customer Man stamped and ranted, the more radiant Karl the Tobacconist's smile became and the slower and more deliberately he puffed on his pipe. For reasons of his own, the purple giant seemed utterly fixated on Friday as a day of reckoning. That was his absolute deadline, the furthest he would allow present affairs to go on. But in reply, over and over in a German accent thick as gear lube in the frozen belly of a Panzer tank on the Russian Front, Karl the Tobacconist repeated, "Ya, ya, Moonday then. We'll have your pipes ready for you Moonday. Moonday, ya?"

These then were the verbal salvos by which their war of wills was waged. For every thunderous "Friday" Angry Customer Man would fire off, Karl the Tobacconist would lob back a nearly inaudible "Moonday, ya, Moonday," the long, slow, extra round vowels in the middle of the first workday of the week stretching it phonetically all the way back to its astrological origins. And slowly, as Angry Customer Man got himself good and blustered out, he came to understand in the most profound of ways that Moonday it was going to be.

That day I did stay around long enough to have my little chat about swapping my dirty cigarettes for a nice new shiny pipe. And then I stayed a while longer. For the next two decades I became a fixture at Karl's shop. Over time one new pipe became a three-tiered rack of pipes, and a lasting friendship blossomed. Again and again I'd return to that oasis of a store to experience the intoxicating smell of dark oily tobaccos bleeding their exotic flavors and aromas into one another at the bottoms of large teak mixing bowls. I came back for the relaxing company of men at leisure, more times than not a smoldering pipe in their mouths and a cup of hot coffee in their hand. I came for their stories and their smiles and the shine on their pipes. Strangely, thinking back on it now, I even came back for the plush feel of just vacuumed royal red carpet beneath my feet. But more than anything else, I came back to visit with Karl himself.

Allow me to try a little rogue psychology on you here. It's long occurred to me that most people you meet in the course of a lifetime are all, to some greater or lesser degree, predictable in much the same way celestial bodies are. Think about it. Established science governing mass and distance allows us to predict the location and behavior of damn near every speck of matter in this universe at any particular time. Big matter has big gravity, little matter little gravity. Therefore everything is pulling on everything else in some measurable fashion.

We're told space is infinite. Just think of what sort of world it would be if everything had the potential to go flying off on a lark to unimaginable dark distant places. But they don't, of course, because old measurable, predictable gravity has got its grimy hands into and around everything. Gravity is the traffic cop of the universe. Boring as it sounds, from the biggest to the smallest object in the world, everything has got its orbit to run, steady and reliable as clocks.

Now think of the people you know. Again, human potential might at first glance appear to be as limitless as space, an infinite galaxy of personal choices from which to decide. But I would propose to you here that people have gravity too. Sure, sure, big people have big gravity and little people little gravity. But all the humans I know think of themselves as being interconnected by laws of acceptable behavior that pull on us all. Planets have their gravity, and people their laws of civility.

Are these laws real in any absolute sense or are they only made up? It would seem not to matter, because in the end, when examined closely, it can be seen that in an illusionary world of infinite choice, real or imagined, they render us utterly predictable. Know a person long enough and well enough, and you can actually chart their orbit. To know what a human being will do today, it is usually only necessary to know what he did yesterday. Sure, sure, the wild and crazy, the rebels among us, they may have grander arcs and further to travel before even they too must inevitably begin repeating themselves. But it would seem the laws by which we've agreed to live our lives have rendered us all profoundly predictable. One to another, each of us has a self-prescribed orbit to run.

Having said all this, amongst constellations there is the exception. Those professionals that map the heavens call such rare phenomena supernovas. Something heats them up or blows them up, and kaboom, they are away, set free from the shackles of gravity to careen according to their own mass and speed and dictates to any place in the galaxy they care to go. In nature's perfectly circumscribed coloring book, they are the scribbles outside the lines.

If you watch closely, you'll see people like this as well. They're rarer than hen's teeth but they do exist. If you're lucky you might encounter one in a lifetime. In my lifetime, that one human supernova was Karl the Tobacconist. In a world of human clocks, my friend Karl could be a piano one day and a carousel the next. That was his special gift.

How'd Karl get himself that way? What river of nature has the force to cut a permanent smile into the face of a man? What heats a man up or blows him up and sends him careening? In the case of Karl the Tobacconist it was war. Seated in the deep leather chairs he kept stationed before his great bay window full of smoking paraphernalia, house blend burning nicely in our pipes, Karl the Tobacconist revealed the secret of his astounding serenity.

As a teenager Karl slept in a boy's bed in his mother's home. Seems he was quite an athlete. Every hamlet in Germany big enough to have a general store and a post office had a soccer league. In his town Karl was the star player. He was smaller than most, but what he lacked in size he made up for in speed. Then World War II began. An infantryman now, Karl found himself passing his nights in an army cot too short for his feet. Days were spent marching across one too many exposed fields somewhere in northern France. Hidden machine guns opened fire. Within chaotic seconds half the men in Karl's company, including Heinz Mueller, his boyhood friend since grammar school, were dead. Karl's lieutenant, an aloof fellow nobody particularly liked or trusted, began shouting, "Get down, get down!"

As luck would have it, at that moment Karl was standing in the middle of a rutted road. When he threw himself down, he found himself lying on his back in the long deep footprint of some French farmer's tractor. Bullets from enemy machine guns zipped and zinged just over his head, but if he kept himself compressed in his furrow it seemed they could not find him.

But Karl was not alone, and not every German who'd thrown himself down had been lucky enough to find a protective hole. The killing bullets seemed to be everywhere. The way Karl told it, "a whole bunch came so close to my chest the little zinging tunnels they furloughed in the air raised the button flap on my shirt." Men were dying all about. A soldier Karl could not see lay so near he could hear his ragged breathing. He was softly moaning for his mother. "Mutter, mutter, mutter." Then came the sound of three short bursts, "thump, thump, thump," and the man moaned no more. And now the aloof officer no one liked or trusted was calling, "Get up, get up, everyone advance to the wall!"

At that very moment Karl's rectum let him down. Lying face up, the warm Mediterranean sun scorching his unprotected eyes, he soiled himself. Yes, Karl heard the order to advance. But like he said to me over those pipes in those comfortable chairs by the window, "how does one get up and run and at the same time go to the bathroom?" So Karl stayed where he was and finished his business. And when he finally did get up filthy, embarrassed and afraid, hands above his head ready to surrender, every other man in his company was dead. Diarrhea had saved Karl's life. The string of strange ironies that would shape his future character had begun.

Karl was taken prisoner. In England, men too old or unfit to serve in the military organized their own soccer leagues. Problem was, with the military being desperate for fresh bodies, there were precious few elderly or unfit sportsmen left behind to kick balls. So some genius in Whitehall came up with the idea of conscripting German POWs with soccer experience to fill out the slim rosters. And so it was that Karl was transported under guard to England from France, given a fresh uniform and instructed to play soccer.

As a star, he was feted in four-star English hotels and palatial homes wherever he traveled. In the mornings he'd awake in four-poster beds, covered chin to toes in the finest cotton sheets. Breakfast would be served to him on a tray in bed. Often a complimentary English paper would come with the meal. In it Karl could read all about the ongoing carnage over on the Continent, numbers of men killed and maimed, battles won, battles lost. Then he'd shower and suit up in soccer shorts for his afternoon match.

With his customary smile, Karl put it to me this way. "The insanity of it all did me in. I haven't been the same man since." And so, I suppose, are human supernova created.

The last time I spoke to Karl the Tobacconist was in the hospital the day before he died. A physically vital man still in his fifties, he'd had the unfathomable bad fortune to suffered a massive heart attack. In his antiseptic room we sat again side-by-side before a window, its claustrophobic little sill a total stranger to the flash and grandeur of smoking paraphernalia on display. The chairs were not made of soft leather. There were no pipes. Just good talk between old friends. This was on a Wednesday.

When I got up to leave, I assured Karl I'd be back again to see him Friday. That seemed soon enough. For you see, I was a foolish man who only knew how to set his watch to well-person time. Karl's gaunt face lit up with a tired half-smile. "Ya, ya," he whispered holding my hand, "Moonday. I'll see you Moonday." The next afternoon Karl's wife called to tell me he had passed.

The story of Karl the Tobacconist has been woven into the fabric of my family's history. It's part of our parlor lore. When company comes and drinks are served, it's always there for the telling. My wife and kids know it by heart. One to another, we use Karl's word "Moonday" often. It's code, you see. For us it's come to mean that bittersweet eighth day of the week that never quite dawns, the missed opportunity that can't be made up. "Ya, ya, Moonday" we say about something we know we'll never quite get around to. We say it and we smile.

Honest As Briar

If you've read any of my pipe stuff, you might know of my special affection for "old guys," pipes that are grizzled and caked from use. Why others might value shiny new pieces is not lost on me, and if suddenly every old pipe in the world were to up and disappear, I suppose I too would smoke new. But given a choice, I'll take a Humphrey Bogart of pipes over a Brad Pitt pipe every time. Why? My theory is this. Usually the most used pipes are the most loved, and usually love of pipe is a direct result of how a pipe smokes. So when I see cake bubbling over the rim of a briar and the blast worn smooth by the caress of a human hand, I'm thinking maybe I've found my treasure.

So anyway, this morning I'm smoking maybe my favorite pipe, a seventy year-old Charatan sandblast that's been hand-rubbed damn near smooth with use, and I'm looking at an on-line photo of Bill Unger, the much loved and recently deceased editor of the Pipe Collector newsletter. I think the photo is one Maxim Engel may have taken at Bill's last NASPC show. Bill is standing down after a long day of hosting and pipe hawking. He's tired but visibly happy, a giant billiard sticking from his mouth. And the unexpected image that came to my mind was this. If they were to attempt to make a movie of my Charatan, and Bill was an actor, he would be perfect in the role of my much beloved, near worn out with use pipe. Bill's face in the photo is the human personification of all things I love in old briar, an honest good thing worn down by loving use to a point where the inner beauty shines through.

As Luck Would Have It

It was the afternoon of the night before Christmas. The party at the office had been a gas. Now I was driving home with some smokin' John Coltrane on the radio and peace in my holiday heart. I was happy in the way a guy gets when he's got a few pops under his belt and there's nothing further needs doing. The tree was up. Gifts for the wife and kids were long since wrapped and hiding in my closet. I'd even remembered to stop by Discount Liquors and pick up the obligatory bottle of Chambord for the wife's stocking—god bless her selfish little heart.

It should have been straight home from there. Thoughts were of another cocktail and maybe even a romantic "nap" with the old battleaxe. But as luck would have it, my journey took me by the brightly striped awning of the Orange Calabash, my local brick and mortar. Not an easy place to get past, the Orange Calabash. It's more-or-less my home away from home. For thirty-odd years I've been just stopping by that little tobacco shop for no reason other than just loving to do it. So I can't say I was surprised when my car just kinda pulled itself up to the curb and turned itself off in front of its familiar beckoning door.

Theodore "Doc" Kincade is the long-time proprietor of the Orange Calabash. Doc and I go way back. But lately something strange has been going on with that man. Ever watch one of those el cheapo made-for-television movies where people can change into anything they want? Shape shifters, I think they call them. Well, lately I'm thinking Doc Kincade may be one of them. Because after almost a quarter century of lovingly restoring old pipes in that little cubbyhole of an office of his, it's undeniable that Doc's begun to look just like those battered briars he keeps pushing into his buffing wheels. Shaggy-headed, unkempt, rumpled as a bag of dirty laundry, through some unfathomable alchemy of occupational intensity, Doc Kincade seems well on the way to becoming the human equivalent of an unrestored estate pipe.

He's also about the closest thing to a brother I've got on this planet. For more years than either of us care to count, Doc and I have been sharing bowls of strong English tobacco together. There've been bowls to celebrate the good times in our lives and bowls to get us past some bad ones. But always, steady and dependable as sunrises in the mornings and dustups with the Queen of My Existence at night, there've been those bowls. The quarter-inch thick cakes that blister up and over the rims of the few pipes I keep stationed at the Orange Calabash will attest to that. Old carbon never lies.

My thought, if I'd had one, I suppose, had been to make a beeline for the backroom and pull down one of those old smoking veterans. After loading up with something tasty from one of Doc's big apothecary-style glass jars with heavy knob-handled lids, I'd settle into one of the leather armchairs positioned by the front window. Then, when Doc got around to joining me, we'd strike our wooden matches in unison and get down to some serious pipe puffing. In the Church of the Orange Calabash, this was our habit, our ritual, our sacrament.

But as luck would have it, just like I was a hungry raptor circling a perfect meadow of tall mice and short grass, something in the presentation case at the back of the shop caught my pipe collector eye. In the week or so since I'd last been in, apparently Doc had gotten in a few new estate pipes. I'd be willing to swear one, a big bent billiard with a nice craggy blast, was, if shape and execution meant anything, an old Sasieni. But was it a family piece or something newer and far less intriguing? There was no telling. Because even a hungry raptor can't spot the difference between a florid fishtail-shaped Sasieni signature and a bland machine-scripted one when the pipe in question is facing the wrong way under locked glass.

That old familiar pipe collector anticipation hit me like a drug, the powerful rush of not knowing but hoping, hoping against all hope and all common sense that somewhere out there in a post-eBay desert of picked over pipes and vulture collectors, the blessed oasis of an overlooked marvel of a pipe might still exist. If I'd let them, my silly pipe collector feet would have danced a nervous jig of anticipation. Instead, I turned to ask my old buddy, Doc, if we might take a closer look at those hidden stampings. But again, as luck would have it, at the same instant another customer grabbed his ear.

Now that I think about it, the portly fellow now consuming Doc's full attention had been pacing back and forth in the front of the shop when I'd walked in. I hadn't paid him any mind. Perhaps I should have. 'Cause now I marked his appearance as being eccentric in the extreme, even for a customer in a tobacco shop. I mean, ever notice how at times every blessed pipeman left on Earth seems to be sporting some variation on a scruffy wild man beard? And what's with that thing that happens to human eyes when the person looking through them has been obsessing for an ungodly long period of time over wooden smoking icons sculpted from the bulbous roots of Mediterranean shrubs? Those eyes seem to glow somehow. Ever notice that? But even by those macabre pipeman standards, the mystery guest in the Orange Calabash this particular Christmas Eve afternoon seemed clearly outside the norm.

For one thing, he had unnaturally thick facial hair. The fields of his cheeks seemed literally planted in silvery stubble. This coarse crop was bounded on the north by plumes of longer, wilder whiskers that traced the outline of his eyes, twin muttonchops running like snowy rivers across the tops of his ruddy cheeks and then down into a sea of theatrically waxed mustache. A second perpendicular line of bristled whisker, this one lying south of the mouth and centered on the lower lip, hung like a spectacular gray vine. Up and over the chin it popped like a blossom, before taking a daredevil's dive into his Adam's apple.

His clothing left little doubt that in his mind this furry-faced chappie was on safari. There was, of course, the obligatory checked flannel shirt from Abercrombie & Fitch that men of imaginary action all sport as an unofficial uniform of sorts. Worn over this was a loose-fitting and perfectly ridiculous khaki vest, its prominent ammo loops all conspicuously empty. From the belt down the mystery guest was a perfect Papa Hemingway replica, his baggy cargo pants pleated and pressed to a knife's edge, wool-lined cuffs turned up at the boots. And, just in case an awed admirer might still be missing the point that New Jersey was not this most exceptional fellow's natural habitat, the jungle illusion was provided its exclamation point with a sporty broad-brimmed bushman's chapeau and knotted bandana. In Safari Man's sun-reddened little hand, he held a plastic shopping bag.

"No big deal," I remember thinking. "Probably a routine return or exchange. Won't take a seasoned pro like Doc Kincade but a minute to process and expel this pompous chump. Then we'll launch a full-scale Sasieni florid fishtail investigation."

"What I have here," Safari Man began, "is a pipe clearly marked 'imported briar.' It was presented to me in celebration of a special occasion by a very dear friend. A handsome pipe, I think we can agree. But as you'll notice if you examine it closely, there is a hairline crack that's developed just here where the bowl and the long stem part of the pipe come together. It doesn't seem to have any negative effect on the way the pipe smokes, thank heavens, but still, I'd prefer it not be there."

Now like I've said, when it comes to servicing the needs of his customers, my buddy Doc is a consummate professional. It takes a lot of hard burrowing to get beneath his leathery hide. Still, it may just have been my imagination, but something in Safari Man's demeanor seemed to have my man a little off his game.

"What exactly is it you'd like me to do for you?" Doc asked, contemptuously examining the nondescript, unstained and utterly fill-riddled pipe in Safari Man's hand, whilst at the same time attempting to generate the prerequisite enthusiasm for a little half-smile.

"Well, you are a pipe-selling professional, are you not? As such, I should think what I want would be quite obvious to you. No pipe made with imported briar should ever crack. I'm certain you'd agree with that. I can only assume my generous-to-a-fault dear friend must have paid an arm and a leg for such a pipe, thinking, no doubt, he was purchasing an object of some quality. I should think the existence of this crack is proof positive that he was mistaken and that this pipe was not at all what it was represented to be."

"You'll forgive my asking again," Doc continued courteously, still doing his best to hold up the now visibly sagging ends of his forced smile, now cradling Safari Man's near-to-worthless pipe in his own hand as though it were a Charatan Coronation, "but what exactly is it you feel I should do for you?"

"Why, offer to buy it back, of course!"

The smile on my friend's face collapsed like a suspension bridge constructed of Popsicle sticks. "Did your dear friend buy this pipe in my store? To be honest, I don't recognize this piece of merchandise as anything I've ever sold. The pipes you see in the store, even the inexpensive ones, are all made by companies who stand behind their workmanship, who guarantee their pipe to me so I can guarantee them to you. Why . . ." And here Doc made a move to pluck one of the least expensive pipes in his shop out of a basket resting on the display case. But Safari Man was having none of it. He interrupted.

"Surely, sir, you don't mean to imply that this pipe, my pipe, a pipe clearly marked 'imported briar' and given to me by a most generous friend of long standing, is in any way comparable to pipes such as these?" Saying this, Safari Man pointed a small red finger at the basket. In it were what I'd always thought to be a rather nice assortment of inexpensive but very presentable starter pipes. Unfortunately for Doc, there was also a small sign in the basket. It read ALL PIPES IN THIS BASKET TEN DOLLARS OR LESS, FREE POUCH OF HOUSE BLEND TOBACCO INCLUDED!

""Well, sir, yes, I was about to offer you a free exchange. Your pipe, a pipe I did not sell and therefore didn't make a penny on, for any one of these nice little basket pipes. They're all made of imported briar, just like your own. Plus each of these has been given what any good pipe really requires, a lovely stain and finish."

Perhaps the Christmas spirit was upon him. Perhaps Doc too had already had a few holiday pops and was just in the mood to be magnanimous. The deal he was offering seemed insanely weighted in favor of Safari Man, an ignorant buffoon who, in my humble opinion, didn't have a haggler's leg to stand on. The old Doc, the Doc I thought I knew, would have shown this bum the door long ago. Where all his newfound patience and generosity were coming from, god only knows. But to me, a man with a mind gone feverish with Pipe Acquisition Disorder and a lingering hope of still salvaging that romantic "nap" before the "what do you think mom and dad are up to in there?" Kid Squad kicked down our bedroom door, it was all taking much too much time.

And I wasn't the only one thinking along these lines. As the clock ticked off unredeemably lost quarters of an hour, a number of other pipemen, some familiar to me, some not, had shown up. After all, it was Christmas Eve day. What pipeman doesn't want a tin of his favorite tobacco or that shiny new pipe for Christmas? If Santa won't bring it, well, then you gotta bring it yourself. These are just hard and familiar facts about Christmas that every pipeman comes to know. So now, standing behind me was a nice little line of grumbling, pipe-puffing last-minute shoppers. When I turned 'round to see how many there were, "grumble, grumble" was all I could hear, and the rhythmic bobbing up and down of all those pipes in all those tight-lipped grumbling mouths was all I could see. And still the horse-trading between Doc and Safari Man ground on.

"Will you take this?"

"No."

"Will you take that?"

"No."

"How about this then?"

"No, no, no."

Desperate to salvage this last-minute bounty of Christmas sales, to get to the line before every blessed pipeman on it said "enough" and stampeded for the door, Doc played what to me seemed an insane gambit. He offered Safari Man any pipe in his estate collection in exchange for his worthless piece of junk pipe. And I don't mind telling you there were some really quality old puffers in that rack—including my potential Family Era Sasieni bent billiard!

"Here," Doc almost pleaded, pulling an eighteen-pipe rack of beautifully refurbished vintage briars up from inside the glass case, "these are the best used pipes I own. Pick one. Any one. Take it and go. I don't even want your pipe. But please, take one and go."

I held my breath. My mind raced. "No," I thought, "not my Sasieni!" The sloppy handwriting seemed to be well and truly scribbled all over the wall. This was not going to end well for anyone, especially me.

And then, incredibly, to everyone's stunned surprise, poor out-of-his-mind Safari Man issued a final emphatic "no." It came as a blasphemy, an affront to everything that is accepted as gospel about the high art of pipe haggling. It defied all logic. But it was what it was. The crazed man refused Doc's final beyond-generous offer.

"When my dear friend first purchased this quality pipe made of genuine briar in somebody else's store, it was new. I see no reason why I should now have to settle for something in exchange that has obviously been used."

As luck would have it, sitting next to the basket of ten-dollar bargain pipes was the biggest briar pipe any one of us had ever seen. This freakishly large, perfectly-shaped billiard had been berthed like an ocean liner atop that glass case for as long as I'd been coming into the Orange Calabash. It was anchored there at both ends by twin U-shaped rests massive enough to have once cradled the replica whale at the Museum of Natural History. That pipe and those rests were something to see!

The story of that extraordinary pipe, as Doc told it, was this. The Dunhill rep for the New York region back in the Fifties, a dapper little man who definitely fancied both the ponies and the ladies and whose full name may have been either Arnie or Barney Silverman—Doc was never quite sure which—had presented this spectacular oddity to the original owner of the Orange Calabash as a display piece. Button to bowl it spanned three feet or more, a monstrously engorged white-dotted shell briar Dunhill pipe perfect in every respect except one.

In one of the great mysteries of pipedom, its gigantic elephant's—trunk-sized shank had never been bored out. Some days Doc supposed the Dunhill factory might just not have had a twist-bit long enough to do the job. At other times he'd be more philosophical, puffing on his pipe and musing, "I suppose the answer to that mystery died right along with Old Alf Dunhill himself."

Whatever truth there was in anything Doc had ever said now seemed inconsequential, because glancing down, I noticed he'd begun unconsciously throttling this grotesque specimen of the pipemaker's art tightly around its robust stem, just as if it were a sledgehammer or a war club. Reflexively, I collared my friend's wrist with my left hand, using all the downward force I could muster as a safety of sorts against any unintended violence.

More time had passed, and now the line of pipe-bobbing grumblers had grown into an unruly mob. A subdued but unmistakable chant had gone up. Without so much as removing a single pipe from between a single set of clenched teeth, the queued up choir of severely miffed puffers had begun in unison to whisper, "kill the bastard, kill the bastard."

A strange change had transpired. As the unreasonable negotiations had dragged on and on and Christmas Eve grew dangerously nearer and plans and dreams for getting in and out of the pipe shop and still having time for other more festive things had vanished, the nature of time itself had warped. What every pipe-smoking soul on that interminable line, myself included, was now experiencing was time slowed to a deadening crawl. It was the desperate time sick people languishing in hospital beds reconcile themselves to. It was the useless time soldiers in battle confront, time incapable of measuring or recording momentous human tragedy in the inadequacy of fleeting minutes and seconds, the stupid time that causes dead-eyed combat veterans to throw down their watches and weep. It was, in a word, dangerous time.

Safari Man's mysterious intransigence was the catalyst for this subtle but unmistakable transition from unbridled holiday cheer to a palpable fear of impending doom. And yet he alone seemed oblivious to the change.

"I believe you've been patently unfair in these negotiations, sir," he chastised, "and so I believe I shall keep this imported briar pipe my dear friend was kind enough to give me. You may consider the matter of this pipe, as it concerns you, to be concluded. However, I do have one further piece of business I do wish to conduct with you."

With this, Safari Man pulled a baby-blue carton of what appeared to be foreign cigarettes from the same plastic bag into which he'd just returned his pipe. He continued. "My wife was traveling in Europe with a dear friend of the family last summer and purchased these Gauloises Bleues cigarettes. I suppose she was thinking, mistakenly as it turns out, that she'd enjoy smoking them once she'd returned home. I was wondering if you, sir, as a professional seller of tobacco products, might consider replacing them with something a bit more to her liking?"

The line of pipe smokers that now ran out the door onto the sidewalk continued to bob their pipes up and down, still half-chanting, half-whispering "kill the bastard, kill the bastard." But one poor chap in a jaunty cap and smoking what appeared to be a Peterson system pipe now came completely unhinged. He opened his mouth wide and bellowed "KILL THE BASTARD!" In that moment of unbridled fury, his little pre-Irish Republic bent billiard tumbled from between his parted lips, cascading down to explode on the immaculately vacuumed carpet in a shower of spark and curly brown, unburned tobacco shard.

At the front of the line, with no further conscious effort on my part, the safety grip I'd been maintaining on Doc's clenched fist and the three-foot-long, perfect-in-every-detail-but-one Dunhill shell briar pipe relaxed. Up went the gigantic unsmokeable "for display only" sandblasted bludgeon, and down. Safari Man sagged beneath the ferocious application of all that hefty Mediterranean root. In a single clarifying instant of cathartic relief, human bone and brain goop and blood were everywhere, on top of pipes and pipe cases and pipe smokers alike. It was a mess of titanic proportions to be sure.

But as luck would have it, even this grayest of clouds carried with it a silver lining. In the same violent instant that ended so very, very badly for Safari Man, and yes, for my brother-from-a-different-mother, Doc, as well, normal time resumed for every pipe puffing son-of-a-gun on that line. Happily, their grumbling ceased. Christmas was saved.

Thunderclap
From Jell-O

In the two years I've been a regular contributor to the Pipe Collector, I think it fair to say that I've never so much as hinted at any political proclivities I may be suffering from. And that, sure as heck, is not because I don't have any. In those same two years I've read tons of articles by countless fellow contributors. I've purchased archived copies of the Pipe Collector going back to its inception. I've devoured so many issues of this newsletter that its regular contributors feel like old buddies lounging around my house. I've even attended an actual pipe show and spoken to real pipe people. As a result, I've learned a lot about some of you, what pipes you cherish, what tobaccos you smoke. But NEVER, NEVER, NEVER, in the pages of this chatty publication, or out-and-about in the real pipe world, have I ever read or heard a single word about anyone's political sympathies.

So for me, Rick Newcombe's piece in the December issue of this journal warning us about the possible ravages of political discourse upon our beloved hobby came like a thunderclap from a bowl of Jell-O. It all seemed that totally inappropriate. Why, I asked myself, would someone admonish us not to do something that, to the best of my knowledge, we never had?

And then Mr. Newcombe himself provided me with my answer. Like the cop that kills or the priest who hangs headless chickens upside-down in the rectory closet, Mr. Newcombe proceeded in his piece to do exactly what he asks us not to do. He airs his political laundry out for all to see in our heretofore politics-free newsletter. He brings the beast to our banquet. Before Mr. Newcombe is done telling us about how politics can destroy our hobby, we get to hear an earful of pejorative political palaver from the author himself.

Clearly, the villain in Mr. Newcombe's piece is "the nanny state," those who would presume to tell us how to live our lives and smoke our pipes. As prideful pipemen, none of us like being told how and where we can smoke our pipes. On this I think we are all of one mind. But Mr. Newcombe's "nanny state" is not anonymous. It isn't even party-less. Mr. Newcombe gives it a recognizable face. His piece links "the nanny state" and "liberal fascism" in language if not in fact, combining them in one telltale sentence as if they were interchangeable and inexorable linked. Clearly, in Mr. Newcombe's piece, it's liberals who are the freedom-stealers in America.

But strangely (or perhaps not strangely at all), other non-liberal freedom-stealers, men and women possessed of a righteous fanaticism so strong they believe they've been given holy license to preach to the rest of us about how long we must live and how we must die (think Terry Shivo) and who and how we must love (only with members of the opposite sex, for to do otherwise is an abomination, and unprotected, not a single tax payer penny spent on contraception for the mother of ten who's at wit's end), these master priers into people's personal lives do not earn a single reference in Mr. Newcombe's piece. They do not seem to be part of his "nanny state."

What we do hear about is how, at pipe shows, Mr. Newcombe meets all sorts of people. They run the gamut from ". . . individualists who favored freedom above everything else," to "pipe collectors who are very comfortable with the central planners in Washington." Just in case you are brain dead, freedom-loving Americans are always the default good guys in all such political polemics. Who better to champion your cause other than lovers of good old-fashioned American-style freedom "above everything else"? Even, I suppose, when "everything else" is never defined, and might conceivably include things near and dear to other Americans that they might be expected to have to relinquish in the name of another's thirst for their absolute freedom.

For instance, let's say some good guy, in the name of his love of his freedom above everything else, wished to own fully automatic weapons and armor—piercing bullets to jam in their thirty-round magazines. What then becomes of the freedom of the guy who lives next door to this armed-to-the-teeth freedom lover? What if he doesn't want to see his home, or his neighbor's home for that matter, converted into an armory? He just wants to walk the streets of his town free of the fear of being gunned down in a hail of automatic rifle fire and send his kids to school in relative safety.

More guns, less guns, no matter where your sympathies lie, can we not at least, as open-minded pipemen, agree that there might need to be some discussion of what "freedom above everything else" means in a crowded society that we all must share? Where does one's absolute freedom end in America today, and where does another's begin? Can we not at least think about such things? And can we think about them with pipes in our mouths?

In 2002 Mr. Newcombe encounters a young friend. With exacting specificity he explains to this friend what he likes about Paul Ryan. We're told the tasty Ryan bits anyone might be expected to relish. Big, complicated issues are distilled down to dandy-sounding bumper-sticker-sized slogans that might easily fit inside the brain of a simpleton. GOVERNMENT IS TOO BIG. WASHINGTON SPENDS TOO MUCH MONEY. Other less tasty Ryan bits, ones that might stick in the public craw and prove worthy of pipes-in-hand debate, issues like voucherizing Medicare and privatizing Social Security, these are presumably either never discussed or go unreported here. What we do find out is that when it comes time for this young, likable friend of Mr. Newcomb's to defend his position, the anti-Ryan liberal position, the best he could muster was an anemic "he was a phony or some such thing."

For past good deeds, I would like to give Mr. Newcombe a pass here. Might it not be possible to think of him as a verbal sloppy dresser who's simply unaware his political underwear is showing? But what little snippets of Mr. Newcombe's biography I am aware of inform me that he is a wordsmith. He works very successfully with written words for a living. From such professionals sloppiness is not expected. Their words are crafted for effect. And the implication Mr. Newcombe would leave us with here is that those who can still dare to think that "the central planners in Washington" are not necessarily always the problem in a post-Ron Reagan world are, if not less American, at least less able to mount an effective intellectual defense of their basically indefensible positions. "He was a phony or some such thing." Why, this poor, likable, insanely superficial liberal friend of Mr. Newcomb's can barely make himself understood. This, of course, is pernicious nonsense . . . and very clever writing to boot.

Mr. Newcombe would further have us lament the high cost of taxes in socialist nations of the world. Which leads me, as a thinking pipeman, to wonder this. How do those who'd have us adopt an oversimplified view of socialism as a failed system of high taxation reconcile their view with the fact that many of today's thriving socialist regimes are democratically elected? How about that for a hot topic of pipe smoking debate, especially with all that's going on in the Middle East today? Are democratic elections an absolute good in and of themselves, or are they only "good" when we in America concur with their results? Does the Muslim Brotherhood play any better in America now that it's been democratically elected to govern? How about that for a three-pipe-problem?

Or how about this? Let me postulate for the sake of a good pipe smokers' debate that nobody likes paying taxes to any country, no matter what it decides to call its system of government. But they do it anyway, grudgingly but willingly, so long as they perceive that in the long run it is in their best interest to do so. Value for dollar spent. Isn't that what makes for a happy consumer? Socialist countries are selling an expensive commodity. And you know what the capitalists say . . . free education and free medicine ain't cheap. But by-and-large, some socialist consumers seem to think they're getting some bang for their buck. They're voting "yea" with their pocketbooks and their ballots. Can the same thing be said about political consumers right here in the good old USofA? I doubt many members of the Tea Party would concur with that sentiment. Can we dare discuss that with pipes in hand? I suspect Mr. Newcombe would advise not.

Almost finally, let me say this. I dig Clint Eastwood. As an American male I bask in the testosterone of his public persona. Admittedly, I'm not much for the spaghetti movies. I think it's all that wacky spaghetti music that puts me off, or maybe it's those disturbing close-ups of craggy-faced Eli Wallach. But, man, Clint sure can direct! Give the man a script and put him behind a camera and you're gonna get one hell of a movie.

But having said all that, the night a strangely wacky Clint Eastwood stood on the stage of the Republican National Convention and all but put the words (yeah, it was cleverly coded in just the way you'd expect an artist to do it, but we all got the message anyway, right?) "Mr. Romney, go fuck yourself" in the non-profane mouth of the President of the United States, that night Clint Eastwood disgraced himself not only as an artist, but as an American.

Oh, and by the way. The fact that Mr. Newcombe erroneously thinks he heard Mr. Eastwood addressing those words to President Obama does not surprise me. I chalk that one up to pure Right Wing political wish fulfillment. You wish so badly for something to happen that voila, next thing you know, there you are, asserting in print that it actually did happen. A grievous but understandable mix-up. But the fact that Mr. Newcombe would hold up this particular disgraceful moment in our recent political history in an attempt to buttress any position of his own leaves me dumbfounded.

Now, before one of my bright and perceptive pipe brethren attempts to point out to me that I've done exactly what I accuse Mr. Newcombe of doing—politicizing this newsletter—let me save you the trouble. I confess. After agonizing over pros and cons, I've done exactly that with premeditation. Only difference between Mr. Newcombe and myself that I can discern is this. I have not done it under the guise of warning others not to do it. Way I see it, a bunch of pipemen, me included, got sucker punched in the political kisser. I know, bad behavior is bad behavior and two wrongs never make a right. But what the hell, I've swung back anyway.

In my very first submissions to this newsletter, one entitled THE U-BOAT SKIPPER'S GBD, I noted that pipe collecting as a hobby probably wouldn't exist today without the tireless efforts of its stalwarts, men the likes of Mr. Newcombe. Rick Newcombe is the father of the open pipe airway. He is the former American ambassador to the royal court of Bo Nordh. If there were a Mount Rushmore for pipe smokers, I have no doubt Rick Newcombe's handsome face would be chiseled upon it right along with Tom Dunn, Old Alf Dunhill and Bill Unger. But in slanting his article the way he did, I think

Mr. Newcombe caught himself up in the same trap that ensnared Mr. Eastwood. Way I see it, Clint and Rick are both fundamentally good guys who inexplicably did a regrettably bad thing.

There's no way to prove or disprove this, but it passes for conventional wisdom that you never hear the bullet that kills you. Language can be like that too. In the skilled hands of those who use them expertly, words can be as silently deadly as bullets. And these days it seems there are marksmen everywhere. So pipemen, keep your pipes up, your heads down and those mildly nicotine-addicted brains on full alert. Question the words of every writer you encounter everywhere, even (maybe especially) mine.

Good Doggie

Each evening, just before going to bed, I feel myself being yanked into my kitchen just as if I was a hound on a leash. At the master's end of that cruel tether is my commandant brain, ordering me to station myself directly in front of my little four-burner gas stove. And because at heart I'm an obedient doggie and my brain is not somebody a good doggie wants to trifle with, that's exactly what I do. Once there, the ritual never varies. I scan the controls and inspect the burners, hoping to convince myself nothing has been left on. Then, because I can never trust my own lying eyes, I'm compelled to turn each knob on the stove in the direction of "off."

It is a fine line I must walk. On the one hand, I'm required to apply enough pressure to each knob to assure my irrational but incessantly demanding brain nothing is amiss. On the other hand, there is the desperate fear of upsetting my always dangerous wife by applying so much pressure to her precious stove that I land up snapping one of its knobs off in my hand. It may not be brain surgery, but some nights it can feel that way.

Now, if I'm lucky and nothing seems awry, I can try stepping away from the stove. Always, my fervent hope is that my brain is done with me, that now, having done every blessed unnecessary thing it's commanded, I might be allowed to go to bed. But that's not how this game is played. Just as the playful cat is never done with its mouse till it's dead, my stove knob ritual must be repeated ad nauseam, deep into the night until I am exhausted.

You read this and probably think, "This is not an entirely good thing." And I'm inclined to agree with you. Human brains can be unmerciful bullies, and living out one's life as a good doggie, rolling over and fetching and putting out a paw to satisfy the sadistic whims of one's own wits can be a tough row to hoe. But this is me we're talking about here, not you, and just like everyone else in this silly world, for better and for worse, I must live with myself and as myself. And what mental tortures I choose to inflict upon myself in the privacy of my own kitchen in the wee dark hours of the morning are my business and mine alone.

But let's now say I was to write a book, a how-to book on how others ought to behave just before retiring to bed. In it I might relate hair-raising tales about reckless sleepers I've known or simply heard about who audaciously skip all my stove knob shenanigans and simply hit the hay. In my how-to book I might go to great lengths to point out to my fellow sleepers that such foolhardiness poses real dangers to their health. "Nobody is safe," I might stress, "until you have submitted your little stoves to all the rigors of my ritual. Turn those knobs till they crack, people, and when they do, get new ones and turn them till they crack as well. Until you do all that, you'll never be safe in your beds or your minds."

I think we might all agree that in writing such a how-to book (an entirely fictitious book I would never think of undertaking, I might add) I'd have turned a rather nasty corner. In penning such a work, I'd open myself up quite fairly to the accusation that I was confusing my own demon neurosis for a condition others might actually profit from sharing, and of peddling immoderate advice to others in a semi-hysterical tone.

I know, I know. In that little hard-covered book with the golden spine that our parents read to us from as children, Mother Goose famously declares, "what's good for the goose is good for the gander." But Mother Goose, for all her homespun homilies, was not the world's deepest thinker. Hers was, I've always suspected, a rather shallow wisdom that never fails to tickle the ear, but if taken as gospel has the potential to land her disciples in real hot water. And this very propensity for thinking of themselves as the goose and everyone else as gander is the very mindset that tends to wreak havoc on the pages of how-to books, leaching its way into the weaker chapters of even the strongest text.

For instance, one of our most distinguished colleagues has written an eye-opening primer on the art of both pipe smoking and pipe collecting that I would recommend to anyone even mildly obsessed with briar. It is a great read! Within its informative pages the reader is introduced not only to the considered reflections of a master puffer on some of the many vexing challenges of our demanding hobby, but to some of the intrepid men and women who daily pull dusty knots of wood from burlap sacks and, with their bare and extraordinarily gifted hands, transform them into dazzling tobacco-burning works of art.

But I would suggest this. Even the best of books have an annoying propensity for behaving like mirrors that, at unintended times, have a troubling habit of reflecting back upon the person doing the writing. It is a risk anyone sitting down to a keyboard must be prepared to accept. And so there are passages here, in this otherwise most excellent book that gave me pause. Rather than providing me with information pertinent to enhancing my pipe smoking experience, they seem, to me anyway, to present an unflattering portrait of this author as he stands before the madness of his very own midnight four burner stove.

Our esteemed colleague, in a chapter dedicated to estate pipes, quotes a German pipe collector and author who compares smoking a used pipe to "using someone else's toothbrush." Another quote in the same chapter from a Scandinavian pipe manufacturer is "You know if you wet your pants it might feel good for a minute, but then you feel soaked, dirty and in need of a bath and a change of clothes." True, neither of these mega-pejorative quotes comes from the author's own lips, and both are included by him to illustrate a difference in attitudes between American and European pipe smokers, But in reading his own words throughout his otherwise delightful book, it is not difficult to infer where this author's sympathies lie on this subject of pipe cleanliness.

He himself states, "Can you imagine? How could you possibly put in your mouth for many hours over a period of years, a pipe that a total stranger, or many strangers, had put in their mouths over however many years? How is this possible?" To those who've dared to suggest to this author that they perhaps know how to clean their estate pipes before smoking them, his reply is dismissive in the extreme. "They don't. I know this because I have studied a number of those 'cleaned' pipes and been astounded at how filthy they were inside." On the face of it, not an outrageous statement—even if one is left to wonder how this author goes about sneaking peeks at the internals of other people's pipes in such detail. I mean, cleanliness is next to godliness, is it not? So who dares raise his hand in objection when good old-fashioned cleanliness is the candidate being voted upon?

Well, I'd suggest to you that even the best of things when carried to questionable extremes tend to become something less than admirable. Check a stove once before going to bed. Good, sound practice. Check the same stove twenty times, snap a few knobs, and you've accomplished something less. So when it comes to estate pipes, let's examine exactly how "clean" is clean enough for this author? Is it enough to soak the stem in a germ-killing bath of Everclear overnight and then buff it on a wheel until every last vestige of oxidation and human saliva has been transformed into a transparent, sterile sheen? No. Is it enough for him to ream the shank with a razor-sharp bit and follow this up with a heavy dose of that very same germ-eradicating Everclear? Again, no. How about topping all these efforts off with a nice thorough reaming of the cake in the bowl. Have we done enough now? Have we satisfied this author? The answer, it would seem, is still a resounding "no."

To him, "all that scrubbing is not enough to convince me that the pipe is like new. I only want to smoke tobacco through raw wood, as opposed to smoking it through a cleaned up version of someone else's carbon coating. This means sanding the tobacco chamber so that it is just wood—with no coating whatsoever." No coating whatsoever? Am I alone here, people, in thinking this moderate-in-all-other-regards author is suggesting some pretty savage surgery here?

This may sound like sci-fi to some of you puffers, but allow me to float a fanciful construct. To me, if it is possible to think of a pipe as being a sentient being, then cake must be its brain. Is not this mysterious build-up within the confines of the bowl the very place where the "ghosts" of the pipe are believed to reside? And what is a pipe "ghost" if not a memory, a carbon imprint of past performances. Wipe the cake away and, yes, I contend you've obliterated memory. To me, scraping away at the bowl of a seasoned pipe until you're left with raw, naked wood is the briar equivalent of the insane plot of one of my favorite movies, *Brazil*. In that epic mess of a film a dentist's chair and a gigantic vacuum cleaner with snaking corrugated hoses the size of elephant's legs are memorably hooked up to suck a man's personality away.

Do I seem to be overreacting here? Consider this. The ritual the author of this highly recommended how-to book follows in cleaning his own pipes after each and every smoke takes a page-and-a-half to describe. For those needing to know each and every exacting detail of all that is entailed, I encourage them to purchase his book. But his stated goal in subjecting himself to all the rigors he prescribes is this: "The next time I smoke it, I can taste the tobacco just as if I was smoking it in a brand new clay pipe—which is precisely what most expert blenders use to test new tobacco mixtures." I could almost feel the knobs of my stove snapping off in my hand as I read that passage.

So now, at the risk of turning that unflattering writer's mirror well and truly on myself, allow me to confess this. To me, the act of smoking a beautiful estate pipe never conjures up images of brushing my teeth with someone else's toothbrush. I've smoked hundreds of such used pipes that I'd presumed to have been in the mouths of hundreds of strangers hundreds of times. And never once did the thought of incisors or bristles cross my mind.

We're all adults here, so if an anatomical analogy is required to describe the fanciful land my mind travels to whenever I'm about to fire up a drop-dead gorgeous used pipe for the first time, then let's try this one on for size. I might fantasize that I've just had the good fortune of stepping into an elevator with the sexiest woman on earth. Highly polished stainless steel doors close with a near inaudible gliding whoosh. We stand side-by-side now inside a most private and confined space, alone together. For no rhyme or reason I can fathom (I am, after all, an ugly old man) she pulls my face to hers and drives her tongue deep into my mouth.

Does what is happening inside that elevator at that moment, and all that I'm thinking and hoping might be about to happen in that elevator, involve the unsanitary mouths of strangers and germs and risk of communicable disease? Sure. But in this, my wildest dream, do I see it as being in my best interest to have this mystery woman stop what she is doing and all she may be about to be doing, so that I might have her take whatever time she needs to ream and sterilize her mouth with a good swishing of Everclear? The hell I do! I go with it, I accept the subterranean risk that runs like a hidden aquifer beneath most all of life's great pleasures. My chapped old person lips part like gleaming elevator doors in a bustling lobby. I take in the tongue of that willowy, willing woman with the same wild abandon I bring to the act of lighting up my luscious new estate pipes. I take them both into me without question or hesitation as a practiced habit. I accept the calculated risks that attach themselves to damn near everything I find worthwhile in my life, from turning the key in my crazy fast Japanese motorcycle to conceiving children and then sending them out into a world I know to be contaminated with dangers of every imaginable stripe.

And when it comes to smoking pipes that have been repeatedly reamed and cleaned till they resemble clay, I say this. Yes, if tasting tobacco is what you do to pay the rent, this is no doubt the wise path to follow. God knows, professional tasters have been known to do all sorts of wacky things in the furtherance of their craft. Damn, wine tasters spit perfectly good wine out into plastic cups without even swallowing it! But who other than a wine taster wants to drink wine like that? And I most emphatically do not taste tobacco for a living. I smoke pipes for pleasure!

Every pipe in my rack is an individual. Some are lords and ladies. If they could speak, I just know they'd sound exactly like Prince Charles at his drollest. But others are total hobos. They've slept under a railroad trestle or two in their time, passing shared hooch around the smudge pot. I can taste that when I light 'em up. But that is who they are. Like their owner, maybe they are not especially proud of every place they've ever gone and everything they've ever done. But we are who we are, my pipes and I. And when we come together in the sacrament of a smoke, me as high priest and they as much loved serving vessels, all masks come off.

I enjoy the taste of tobacco. You got a couple of good cigars or a tin of pipe tobacco to recommend? Count me in. I'm down with that. But what I love, what infatuates me, what lashes me fast to this crazy hobby of ours is the distinctive taste of PIPE, used PIPE, ghost taste-infested PIPE, PIPE with cake and PIPE with a five o'clock shadow of greenish fuzz on the stem. Yes, when well and truly caught up in the thrall of pipe lust I'll even go smiling for a PIPE with a modicum of gunk plugging up its shank.

And as long as I'm coming clean, let me confess to this as well. I don't shower or ask anyone else to shower before making love. I even prefer my ladies sans perfume. So I sure as hell don't get out the Everclear and reamers before lighting up my hobo pipes.

Is this a disturbing admission? Do I hear the distant sound of pipemen blushing? Well then, so be it. I suppose I'm just an immoderate guy. But I promise you this, my pipe-puffing kinsmen. You'll never catch me putting pen to paper with the intention of instructing anyone in the fine art of anything. After a sixty-odd year stint as ringmaster of this personal circus of a life where the lions stalk the patrons in their seats and the daring young men on the flying trapeze pitch to earth with a sickening repetitive thud, the only instructional I feel qualified to author would have to be a how-not-to manual on just about everything.

"Each evening, just before going to bed, I feel myself being
yanked into my kitchen just as if
I was a hound on a leash."

Three Sisters

Let me make one thing perfectly clear from the outset. I don't collect, nor do I particularly cherish Stanwell pipes. I do, however, dig their corporate chutzpah. I mean, how ballsy is it that Stanwell, a Danish pipe company back in the day when being anything other than English was like having marketing polio, deviously selected an English-sounding name for itself in order to bamboozle clueless Americans into buying quasi-freehands?

And yes, okay, there is something oddly alluring about the way all those pseudo-English pipes brazenly bulge in ways and places stodgy English briar never would. In a market where Dunhills and Barlings are touted as lords and ladies, Stanwell pipes dare to drop their knickers and show a hint of stocking. And in sexually repressed America where even Laura Petrie's miniscule television boobs got the Dick Van Dyke Show a stiff ratings boost, a little titillation will always get you noticed. I know that personally, whenever I find myself involuntarily ogling a particularly comely Stanwell, I invariably think, "If the Pillsbury Doughboy had a hottie for a wife, she'd probably look and feel exactly like this." But one can not collect everything, and I most emphatically do not collect Stanwells.

So as you can imagine, it came as a thundering surprise to me when I found myself placing a Stanwell pipe on my eBay WATCH LIST. "Nothing to get the bowels in an uproar about," I assured myself. Because although in the courtroom of my mind, bidding on and winning a pipe one does not want will get you a felony conviction every time, I'm inclined to be much more lenient with anyone - myself included - who simply places that same unwanted pipe on a watch list. I consider this sort of buzzing around the flower without doing any serious pollinating to be a mere mental misdemeanor. It's a lesser offence in much the same way just saying you're mad enough to kill you wife probably won't get you thrown in the hoosegow, but grabbing a cleaver and actually putting the old gal in the ground certainly will. And still, for sure, to any objective and completely sane third party privy to the legal machinations of my cerebral judicial system, the case of this unwanted Stanwell was troubling indeed.

For instance, once placed under oath, I'd have no choice but to confess that it was not just one Stanwell that mysteriously appeared on my watch list. It was THREE! With a simple click of the eBay SEE SELLERS OTHER ITEMS button, I'd discovered this particular seller, an expatriate Englishman living in Germany, was parting with a trio of beloved old briars. And although the one pipe that initially caught my eye was a lovat-shaped affair with a bulbous hump where the stubby stem joined the elongated shank, in my mind's eye the three up-for-grabs pipes were, by way of their inclusion in a single seller's personal collection, now a set.

Auction day dawned ominously. My sleep the night before had been troubled – never a good sign - and in the morning I felt even more powerless than usual in my daily struggle to keep from embarrassing myself. Considering my self-professed lack of real interest or enthusiasm for Stanwells, with seconds to go I dropped in a startlingly high bid on the lovat and won. Mercifully, all the other Stanwell collecting maniacs in the world seem to have been outside cutting lawns or indoors making love to their wives when the eBay clock struck zero. Because even though my winning offer was substantial by my miserly standards, it was less than half the price I'd committed to paying if the bidding had gone haywire.

But now the second of the three Stanwells on my watch list was set to go off in seven minutes. And my blood was truly up. I'm reminded here of a cracking good line from the movie, Moby Dick. I'm not sure whether it was penned by novelist Herman Melville or screenwriter Ray Bradbury, but it's delivered as poor, mad Captain Ahab orders his whalers back to the Pequod in pursuit of the white whale. The men have been off in their little Nantucket sleighs, killing non-white whales all the merry morning long. And when the pipe-smoking first mate, Mr. Stub, hears his crazy captain's order to lay aside the harpoons and lances and cut all lines, he beseeches, "Ah, Captain, our bloods up, that's all. The men have been killing and it's hard to stop killing when you've been killing steady." Well, I suppose it was much that way with me.

The second Stanwell was a darkly stained stack billiard with unusually thick walls. Stack billiards are circus pipes. I know that. But there was something about those unusually thick walls. Exactly what I did not know. But if the art of selling can be compared to the sport of fishing, then those thick walls were for sure the worm on the hook dangling before my hungry fish mouth. And so, as if it had a mind of its own, down thundered my rogue eBay bidding finger again. Seconds later, stunned, slightly out of breath and deeply mortified by my own deplorable behavior, I'd won the second unwanted Stanwell.

Only one Stanwell remained. With it came a last glimmer of hope that I could in some token way still rein myself in. Again I had the same accursed seven minutes to get a grip. The last pipe of the trio was a Sixten Ivvarson-inspired egg-corn-shaped affair. Its defining characteristic was a briar knuckle jointing its shank at the midway point in a most enchanting way. My seemingly disembodied bidding finger once again quivered ominously above the eBay BUY button. Once or twice it actually twitched and began downward, only to stop. Perhaps it was because this time I had an unexpected ally in my struggle for personal redemption. A little on-the-fly monetary calculating had my PayPal balance at something less than zero. I was, as the poker loser declares, "all in." Surely this total absence of expendable capital could and would break my buying fever. Yet in that padded cell within my mind where the screams of practicality always go unheard, I knew I was incapable of stopping.

Not wanting to advance but incapable of retreating, I did what any clever but clearly irrational person would. I seriously lowballed the last Stanwell hoping to lose. I mean, how could I possibly win with such a ridiculously low bid? But incredibly, almost instantaneously, another accursed eBay screen popped up. Totally misunderstanding my intentions, the upbeat message from my clueless computer hit me with all the savage inappropriateness of a drunken wedding singer at a funeral. CONGRATULATIONS! YOU ARE CURRENTLY THE HIGH BIDDER ON THIS ITEM. Unfuckingbelievable!

In the frantic two ticking seconds left to me, even though I'm a super-secular sorta guy, I prayed to lose. Yes, it's true. In this, my darkest moment of total panic and stunning irrationality, I turned to a supernatural deity I do not believe in for help. Perhaps not surprisingly then, I got none and won anyway. I'd completed my terrible Trifecta. And so ended an insane drama that, if Old Captain Ahab had been sitting at my elbow watching it all play out, might have noted was "rehearsed by thee and me a billion years before the wheel on my computer mouse first rolled."

How best to explain such shoddy human behavior to others? In an e-mail to a pipe smoking buddy of mine in Maryland, I attempted to put a semi-flattering face on the whole sordid affair. What I said to him was this. "In my fevered bidding brain the three Stanwell pipes had somehow inextricably been transformed into sisters. One sister, the prettiest of the trio, I fancied making love to. But as luck would have it, these sisters proved to be inseparable, a real all-for-one-and-one-for-all sibling tag-team. And so, in the end I landed up bedding them all."

Thinking about it now, I suppose there are worse fates that could befall a pipeman.

Pot To Piss In

I've come to a strange place in this long walk with my own mortality. I've begun clearing my closets of clothing in preparation for my now entirely foreseeable passing. It's not a scenario pleasant to contemplate, but in the end, it's one that befalls us all. We're finally dead, the funeral is over and suddenly it occurs to some unlucky survivor, wife, child, a best buddy and his alcoholic wife, that our crap must be gone through and gotten rid of. And by default, that unpleasant task has fallen to them.

That jarring image, of someone standing in my bedroom before my bi-fold closet doors confronting my Rack of Shame, the fish ties and parrot shirts, even the blue, wide-whaled seersucker suit I wore to my wedding, well, it's got me seeing my own wardrobe in a wholly different light. Rather than raggedy strands of colorfully woven thread dangling silent from hangers, I now see each article of clothing in my closet as a potential informant, a witness about to give posthumous testimony as to my bad taste and quirky character.

"Who wears stuff that looks like this?" "I don't remember seeing him in anything as ugly as that." "What sort of sick jerk saves junk like this?" These yet to be spoken words are already ringing in my ears, and I'm not even dead yet. So all my most incriminating clothes are being systematically rounded up and jammed down into tightly sealed black plastic garbage bags. In them they'll be dragged off to the trunk of my car, there to be driven to some desperate last resting place from which unloved clothing tells no tales.

Much the same sort of thing's begun happening with my pipes. Over the course of a misspent lifetime, I've somehow managed to accumulate nearly a hundred of those pesky briar buggers. Many, many more than necessary if you ask me. But they've given me great joy, and according the philosophy of life I ascribe to, anything that gives me great joy and at the same does no great harm to others is to be encouraged. So pipes have come in surprising numbers.

Taken as a whole, they now constitute what I refer to as my "collection." I perhaps use this word "collection" recklessly, having read an article right here in the Pipe Collector, in which a high mucky-muck of the Briar Brotherhood argued persuasively that in order to constitute a "collection," an accumulation of pipes must have a theme or logic to them. This esteemed pipeman asserted that it was not enough for pipes to simply congregate in one place in vast numbers. For pipes to be considered for "collection" status, they had to be related one to another in some intellectually identifiable way. Examples he gave were pipes all stamped with one particular maker's name, pipes originating in one country as opposed to many, even a hodge-podge cobbled together from one beloved shape or grain pattern would do, so long as there was that all-important unifying factor.

My pipes are multi-shaped, multi-grained and representative of pipe manufacturers from as many places on the globe as Carter's got liver pills. To the untrained eye - my own included until quite recently - the wildly divergent pipes I've haphazardly dispersed all about my house, a nondescript clump here, another there, would seem a messy accumulation rather than a "collection" in the mucky-muck's strict sense of that word. If there was a single human idea binding them together one to another, aside, of course, from the fact that there are clearly too many of them, I could not see it. I was as clueless in that regard as the guy who's got a pot to piss in, but for no understandable reason uses it as a hat instead and goes right on pissing on the floor.

Then it finally dawned on me. With only the very rarest exceptions, all my pipes are battered and dull. Their hues are subtly unique, but as a collective palate the range of color they represent is dramatically circumscribed. It spans not much further around the rim of the color wheel than ripe hazelnut at the one extreme to burnt hickory at the other. There isn't a shiny warrior in the brigade. This late-in-the-coming revelation has, I think, provided my unruly pipe hoard with a pedigree worthy of the term "collection." All my pipes, the ones I've kept as opposed to the ones that got passed along, are, I now see, "old men." That is their common denominator.

And it amuses me to wonder if a child of mine or perhaps even a precocious grandchild will come along after I'm gone and be perceptive enough to spot this commonality and say, "Holy cow! My dad/granddad was a collector of 'old man' pipes." So to make their puzzle easier to solve, for the first time ever I've begun weeding out and offering up for sale the few pipes in my collection that are not sufficiently battered and dull. I've recently parted on eBay with a Savinelli Autograph #4 that I owned for nearly half-a-century but seldom smoked. Another lightly-colored shiny boy that stuck out like a sore thumb was a large Castello "egg. In the Great Gatsby, Tom Buchanan derides Jay Gatsby's roadster. He calls it a "circus car." In the flashiness of it beauty, my Castello "egg" always struck me in much that way, as a circus pipe. I'm a simple, unpretentious black coupe sort of guy. As a consequence, the Castello "egg" seldom got taken down and fired up.

In my sales solicitations for both pipes, strange as it might seem, I noted quite honestly that I was parting with both pipes because their condition was simply too good. Even as I wrote the words, I wondered what my potential buyers would make of that.

Made-Up Bill

I find it difficult to write for things....newsletters, literary magazines, you name it. If it's an entity and I'm attempting to cobble some words together for it, I've got problems. So what I do is personalize the process. I generally pick out a name and, if I'm lucky, a photo from the masthead and then proceed, fleshing out what flimsy evidence of human existence I possess, breathing a made-up life into that name and that photo as if I am god. I create a whole fictional person and then write for him/her.

In the case of the Pipe Collector, it was poor old Bill Unger who got himself made up. We never spoke, Bill and I, in person, on the phone or otherwise. For all the personality Bill withheld from the few e-transmissions we shared, he might as well have been a robo-editor. I'd rant and banter. Real Bill would dash off an impersonal reply. "Okay, Ralph, do as you please."

So I did what comes naturally to a writer of fiction. I created Made-up Bill, someone it was easier to work with. Like Real Bill, Made-up Bill was a man of few words. But unlike Real Bill, Made-up Bill was in some mysterious way more enthusiastic, more encouraging. And that worked for me. The pieces came, one after another, every few months for years.

And then Real Bill died. Left unsupported by his flesh-and-blood alter ego, Made-up Bill disappeared as well. And that caused real problems, because even with a franticly overactive imagination, I find it impossible to write for pretend dead people. So it felt for a while like my work for the Pipe Collector must disappear along with Made-up Bill.

But I found another name and face to pour "ralph in jersey" made up life into. The writing continued. When done skillfully, each submission still read as if it was written for everyone, but in truth, they were all penned to and for her, my newest creation. Anyway, the reason I'm telling you all this now is because in the last little while I've had cause to contact this real woman on a matter related to pipedom. Always dangerous business that, mixing reality with fiction.

For instance, in response to my query, it became apparent this woman, this real woman whom I'd mentally co-opted into one of my fantasy creations, had apparently all but given up reading the Pipe Collector over the very same period of time I'd been so diligently and obsessively writing articles in it for her. "Holy drop me through the non-existent floor, Batman!" Only a writer can possibly know how strange something like this can feel, a writer or perhaps a prison groupie who, through no fault of her own, discovers she's been penning love letters to a convict the state executed years ago.

But fear not, my fellow pipe puffers. It would seem I've already weathered this most recent setback to my "create a person" campaign. Already a new candidate for "ralph in jersey" fictionalization is being tested out. If he, and yes, it is a he again this time, lives long enough and continues reading long enough, then perhaps I'll continue writing pipe nonsense long enough to get everything I've got to say here said.

Stub Off Itself

If the Pipe Collector is a regular stop on your reading railroad, perhaps you're already acquainted with ralph in jersey's quasi-cockamamie theory of violent pipe lighting, the one he refers to as his Hill of Fire Method. Benignly stated, it postulates that when initially striking fire to a bowl of pipe tobacco, it is far, far better to overlight the dang thing than underlight it. A bold, but not entirely unreasonable assertion, I think we might agree.

But then, because nothing ralph in jersey ever writes is entirely benign, there is more. Seemingly compelled to do himself one better, he takes a flier and asserts that it is literally impossible to overlight your pipe. It's a reckless notion he champions, one that puts folly to all hope of just passing that wooden stick match over the top of your pipe, taking a few feeble puffs and then expecting to be on your successful way. If ralph in jersey is even half-correct, it just doesn't work that way.

My guess is the cause of this fundamental misconception is the inexplicable fact that many normally clear-thinking pipemen seem strangely incapable of telling the difference between kitchen stoves and briar smoking pipes. The two, I assure you, are very different animals. With the former animal, the one with knobs and racks and bothersome grates needing habitual cleaning, all you've gotta do is wave your wooden stick match over its grease-encrusted burners and voila, you're cooking with gas. With the latter animal, the one made of briar that you stick in your craw and puff upon, the dance of ignition is performed to an entirely different tune. Now you've gotta take that same wooden stick match firmly in your clenched fist, and once well and truly struck, literally beat the piss out of your pipe with its fiery end until you hear that briar of yours yowling in pain and crying "uncle!" It's fight club rough stuff we're discussing here, people, martial arts with a stick match. The Hill of Fire pipe lighting method is not for the faint of heart.

Think you've got what it takes to give it a go? Well, then here's some helpful information. When ralph in jersey lays fire to his pipe, he enjoys thinking of himself as that fearsome torcher of southern cities, old Bill Sherman himself. In his mind, the pipe he now cradles in his mouth is Atlanta, the tinderbox capital of everything his alter ego, Bill Sherman, has marched so long and so hard to destroy. For ralph in jersey, this little exercise in Civil War reenactment works every time. So go ahead. Give it a try. Cloak your brain in Yankee blue and really torch that Johnny Reb pipe of yours. And by all means, if you live south of the Mason-Dixon Line and your regional sympathies lie elsewhere, feel free to think of yourself as Nathan Bedford Forest, and of your pipe as Washington, D.C.. The color of your mental uniform is of no consequence. All that matters is that you come to that initial firing up of your pipe with a war whoop in your throat and murder and mayhem in your heart.

So far, so good? Now, with your war head screwed on tight, when you think your pipe is really lit, when that coin-flat plain of compressed tobacco at the top of your bowl has risen up in a literal cherry bomb of snapping fire, when you switch off the lamp in your smoking room and just beneath your nose you're shocked to observe the fearful specter of an erupting volcano, torch it again. That's right. You heard me. Torch it again. Because remember, according to ralph in jersey's quasi-cockamamie theory of pipe lighting, you can not possibly overlight your pipe. Not even when the top of it literally bursts into flame.

And when the Hill of Fire pipe lighting method is practiced as prescribed, at times the top of your pipe will indeed actually combust. But not to worry. Experience has taught ralph in jersey that only the very uppermost fraction of your pipe is likely to be lost in such conflagrations, even under the most savage lightings. With a practiced hand and a trusty spray bottle at the ready, bothersome flare-ups can easily be extinguished when properly anticipated. For the seasoned pipeman, flame at the rim should be considered a non-event, a happening of no great consequence than a creak in the attic or a smudge on a wine glass. No big deal!

In one of his favorite motor racing books, the great Phil Hill, America's only World Driving Champion, is chaperoning a journalist from the airport in Marinello, Italy, to the Ferrari test track outside town. He's doing over 250kph in his blood-red Ferrari road car. The back end jumps out unexpectedly rounding a particularly daunting curve in the road. A quick flick of Phil's practiced wrist, the smallest correction to the steering wheel and the rear end snaps back into line. The careening journey continues without loss of life. The great Phil Hill turns to the scared shitless journalist buckled up beside him and says, "Little things like that don't even tickle my stomach anymore." That spirit, the Phil Hill spirit, is the one ralph in jersey demands of anyone with balls enough to attempt his Hill of Fire pipe lighting method. Douse those flames. Calm the burn with a few slow, deliberate puffs. Proceed to enjoy your pipe. And if you, like ralph in jersey, idolize Grand Prix racing drivers, you can say to yourself as he often does, "The great Phil Hill would be proud of me."

Now hearing all this, the fussy collector-types among us, those dilettantes within the briar brotherhood who value the cosmetic integrity of their precious "art pipes" over the joy of a properly struck smoke, will no doubt get their knickers in a twist. Over the internet miles I detect faint echoings of their communal lament. "Oh, oh, what about the blackening of our pristine rims?" In response to their choir of angst, ralph in jersey simply says, "Rims be damn. Pipes be damned." All that matters is the quality of one's smoke. Sure, as with the pursuit of all great pleasures, there is a price that must be paid. If truth be told – and by way of confession, in ralph in jersey's mind it seldom is – I do not have a single pipe in my rack that does not look like a dwarf with his head burned off. The tallest pipe bowl left standing in my three-tiered Decatur rack measures something less than one inch from rim to bowl bottom. Every briar I own has been rendered a blackened stump of its former self. Once shiny rims have been reduced to jagged fire-forged plateaus of scorched wood cinder. But oh, what wonderful smokes I have enjoyed with each and every one of these truncated briar mutants!

In the end, as I see it, it comes down to this. In spite of any words I might offer up in my own defense, the prissy pipe preservationists will still insist that what I'm suggesting is a travesty. This, I suppose, is to be expected. Members of the Audubon Society don't go around shooting ducks on the weekend. You're unlikely to stroll by a Vegan restaurant and spot blood-smeared diners chewing ravenously on raw steak. The laws of nature we've all consented to live our lives by mandate certain likely outcomes for predictable behavior. ralph in jersey is a realist. He doesn't expect "art pipe" collectors to suddenly go traipsing off willy-nilly, smiles on their faces, merrily burning the tops off their expensive acquisitions in the interest of great smokes. That's just not who they are.

But when it comes to the thorough lightings of my own pipes, I tend to take a more circumspect view of the matter. I'm both heartened and bolstered by the memory of those hearty old nineteenth century seadogs who went a whaling out of all those wharfy little New England harbors. Nautical mayhem was the order of the day back then. But those brave-hearted sons of the sea accepted their whale-bone legs and grappling hook hands as badges of honor, visual testament to a willingness to make the necessary sacrifices in order to earn one's daily bread in a demanding profession.

I think it's much the same with pipes. Until a briar has lost its rim to flame, to me it's but a Pip the cabin boy of a pipe, a half-witted youngster yet to earn its sea legs. So when it comes time to sit back and enjoy the tobak, give ralph in jersey a Captain Ahab of a pipe every time, an old salt who's pulled an oar and cast a lance, a scarred briar forged by the manly ritual of repeated conflagrations and savage lightings. In short, a pipe that's a Stub of itself.

Ship In A Bottle

I recently received an e-mail from a fellow contributor to the Pipe Collector. In it I was mildly chastised for missing the "something specials" he endeavors to put into each and every one of his submissions. That caught my attention, because I too pride myself on attempting to imbed little bonus extras into my pipe pieces. Nothing earth shaking, you understand. Trinkets and bobbles really. In one story it might be a particularly well-honed phrase, in another nothing more than a silly word I'd been hoarding away waiting to unveil. But the thing is, small as they may be, I do know they are there, and although I've never quite thought of them as "something specials," I do secretly pride myself on their inclusion.

What does all this have to say about writers in general and me in particular? Well, if beaten around the head, I'd likely confess to thinking of all writers as being a pack of Willy Lomans. We're out there with our salesman's sample cases brimming over with what we hope are bonus inclusions, but in truth, we're all of us just one evolutionary rung up from conmen and shysters. Our mental wellbeing dangles like a tooth on a string, each one of us a single smudge of the hat away from the little rubber pipe in the basement. I mean, if our readership fails to find or appreciate those nebulous little verbal gifts, what then? Minus fan affirmation, how can we be sure they are really there?

Faced with such daunting uncertainty, all writers rely on emotional crutches to get ourselves around. Here's what works for me. I've measured my talents as a writer against the reception my printed words have received over a long stretch of time, and determined them to be small indeed. So I work small. May the patron saint of pipe smoking forgive me for saying this, but now, when I sit at this desk and clatter away preparing my next packet of pipe words, I see myself as a hobbyist constructing a ship inside a bottle. It is small work being performed by a small man possessed of small talent. But the small task he has set himself to is almost exactly commensurate with his ability to complete it. If I look closely I can see a small pipe in the small man's mouth. When I look more closely still, I see that he is smiling.

Messianic Vision

Last night, ralph in jersey had a messianic vision. Or at least it felt like one. For you see, ralph in jersey is by his own admission a stupid smart person. Most of the thoughts that arrive uninvited in his head are, well, let's be kind here and call them "unique." To hear him think, one might easily be fooled into considering him someone special. In truth, nothing could be farther from the truth. Most days, months, even years, the poor devil hardly thinks at all. And then, when information of the type any clear-thinking person would simply slough off as just another thought arrives in his mostly dormant head, it feels to ralph in jersey as if he's had a "messianic vision."

Case in point. Last night, a full year delayed from when the thought should have arrived, ralph in jersey awoke at three AM, sat bolt upright in bed, and swears he heard the patron saint of pipe smokers tasking him to make damn sure that he does everything in his power to insure that that the late and much lamented Mr. Bill Unger be officially designated a Doctor of Pipes at this year's Chicagoland Pipe Show.

But here's the thing. ralph in jersey has no powers in such affairs. He's never been to Chicago, much less Chicagoland. He has no earthly idea how one goes about becoming a Doctor of Pipes. Is their a doctoral program offered someplace for such things, or do such farfetched titles simply fall from the sky? Aside from one or two fellow collectors he's exchanged occasional e-mails with over the last few years, most of them contentious, ralph in jersey, a lone wolf if ever there was one, has never so much as spoken to a fellow pipe collector, much less a Doctor of Pipes or anyone who's ever even known a Doctor of Pipes. And still, he has by his own estimation now been tasked with drumming up support for the posthumous awarding of an honor he knows nothing about to a deceased individual he never met.

Needless to say, he needs help. His hope is that that out there in Pipeland somewhere there are likeminded Stupid Smart People, who, upon reading this, will feel similarly compelled to make this thing happen. Among them will be someone who can tell ralph in jersey who makes such decisions for the Brotherhood and how they might be contacted. Maybe even the very person or persons charged with bestowing the honor in question will read this note and feel obliged to get in touch. And together we will somehow make this most just and compelling thing happen.

You've perhaps noticed that nowhere in this piece have I made any sort of detailed case for Mr. Bill Unger's elevation to Doctor of Pipes. Perhaps you find that strange. I know I do. But the patron saint who woke me at three AM assured me no such case need be made. I was instructed that if you knew of Bill and his works and love pipes, then you are already on the side of the angels in this matter.

So let's get this done, people, for Bill's sake and our own. Don't know about the rest of you, but a full year has passed since Bill's sudden passing and I'm still hurting badly at the loss of this good man who did so much for all of us. If you believe in such fanciful things as "Doctors of Pipes," then surely you know in your heart that Bill Unger was one of them. Let's give the man the award he earned so we can all start feeling better.

Madly Signaling No-Goodniks

Now what's with all those oddball estate pipe sellers on eBay who insist on taking photos of bent pipes with the stems turned upside-down? You know the ones. The pipes being offered all look like inverted kiddy slides in a funhouse mirror. And it's not just one isolated seller we're discussing here. Scan the columns of pipes offered on eBay long enough and hard enough and it begins to feel like there's an epidemic of these misassembled oddities out there.

Which leads me to wonder if these strange sellers might not be trying to signal something in photographic code. Perhaps the subliminally message we're expected to receive is that, oh, this seller must know nothing about smoking pipes. But how little does a person have to know about smoking pipes to not know in which direction the curved stem is suppose to face?

Okay, yes, we all dream of buying a priceless smoking treasure from an uninformed dunce for a fraction of its actual value. But do any of us really ever want to acquire a pipe, no matter how damn nice and how damn cheap it is, from a complete bumbling simpleton? Would any of us dare exchanging saliva with such a creature? I think not. So I personally suspect something deeper and more sinister may be afoot. I think that as a community of collectors we may have been unwittingly infiltrated by a coven of madly signaling no-goodniks. I'm sensing clandestine tomfoolery, something akin to all those double agents and moles slinking around behind the Iron Curtain stashing empty cigarette packs in the hollows of midnight trees. Is it not possible something very similar may be happening now, right under our very noses and dangling pipes? Just wait and see if time and history don't prove me right!

Mr. Cannabis

For some time now I've been buying just about every estate pipe offered up by one particular seller. Not all of them are pleasing to my eye, but they all smoke very well indeed. As is my habit, I've followed up by e-mail, hounding this individual with questions about the history of my newly acquired pipes. Yesterday, in an e-mail out of the blue, my mystery seller offered up this confession. Seems both he and his brother are lifelong pot smokers. Now if I was the FBI, I'm sure I'd care about this. But I'm not, and I don't. The dead-eyed mopes with badges who've seen fit to throw a lot of gentle people in prison for what amounts to not much more than a little harmless personal recreation are no friends of ralph in jersey. Personally, I was forced to give up weed pretty much right out of college. Flat-out couldn't afford it, what with the wife and kids and all. Well, the kids are gone now, and you'd think my old college pal, Mr. Cannabis, and I would have some catching up to do. But no such luck. Kids or no kids, at a zillion dollars an ounce or whatever obscene amounts they're charging for the stuff these days, weed is a train that's financially left my station for good.

Not so, it would seem, for my estate pipe seller and his brother. Not only can they still afford the stuff, but if their e-mail can be believed, they use it to break in all their new pipes. You heard me. For the first several months of use, the only thing they cram in all those virgin briar bowls is cannabis. Then presumably a new briar is purchased and put to similar usage, while the now broken-in pipe is put out to pasture in the service of English tobacco. Not your usual method of initiating a new briar, I think we might all agree.

But here's the thing. Like I've already noted, ALL the smoking pipes I've purchased from these potheads over what's been an extended period of time have been exemplary smokers. And before you ask, no, their pipes do not seem possessed of pot ghost tastes. Even after my long hiatus, I still recognize a pot ghost when I meet one. And if there are any in these pipes, they've managed to dematerialize beneath an iron-clad ring of tobacco cake. For it would seem that whatever these miscreant brothers decide to smoke in their pipes, they smoke it in excess.

So there it is, pipe puffers, something to contemplate – dope in the Dunhill. I'm not saying it's good for your briars. For that matter, I'm not even suggesting it's good for you, although I'm not prepared to say it isn't. I'm just reporting the facts as I know them for your thoughtful, pipe-puffing consideration.

Then You Wake Up

It was the wrought iron hoop that caught my eye, one of those jobs you stand up next to your fireplace to keep stacks of unruly firewood from rolling all over a living room. This particular hoop's salad days were over for sure. It was sitting abandoned at the curb, the front man for a nondescript pile of somebody's junk.

As I pulled over to get a closer look, I attracted the attention of the "somebody" in question, a gray-bearded gentleman in leather gloves leaning on a rake. Not wanting to seem rude, but at the same time having no inclination to strike up a conversation, I hailed him with a terse "hello" that seemed spot-on for addressing a perfect stranger whose trash I was about to rummage through.

But Old Leather Gloves was the ferociously overfriendly sort. In less time than it took me to determine his fireplace hoop had died and gone to rust heaven, he was on me. Without so much as a single additional word of provocation on my part, the old geezer launched into a wordy and most unwelcome dissertation on his recent family history as it related to the indoor burning of wood.

"When the kids were small we'd loved to burn a fire, blah, blah, blah, and now they've all got homes and kids and fireplaces of their own, blah, blah, blah, and god knows when this thing was last used, blah, blah, blah." And on he went.

I'd stumbled upon a real heap of woe, a chatty old canary swathed in a cloak of loneliness as eye-catching as the flannel shirt on his back. It didn't take a detective to figure out that the wife he failed to mention, the mother of those kids who were once small and now big and in possession of fireplaces of their own, blah, blah, blah, was in all likelihood no longer around to keep him company.

I had places to go and things to do. But I've got a definite soft spot for the old ones, and sometimes, when an emotional trap springs shut on you, the best thing to do is not struggle. So I punched myself off the invisible clock that drives me through my tightly scheduled workday and began making small talk with Old Leather Gloves. Mostly he talked and I listened. But when could get a word in edgewise, I told him a few things I thought he might wanna hear about my wife and kids and our fireplace. Did our little talk make him happy? I don't think so. But I believe for a few minutes anyway I was able to keep him entertained.

Then, just about the time I was fixing to climb back into my van, the hands on that invisible clock always ticking, Old Leather Gloves noticed my pipe. "I got a few of those around here someplace," he sorta whispered more to himself than to me, pointing at the battered briar bowl dangling from the half-open pocket of my jacket.

"My father-in-law was a big pipe guy back in the day. Never remember seeing Pop without one of those silly contraptions dangling from his lips. Pop's gone twenty years or more now. Still have his pipes around here someplace. Let's see? Last I saw 'em they were in the garage. Always meaning to get rid of those smelly old relics, but somehow never do. Funny how things like that happen…know what I mean?"

Now here's the thing. On the wall above the desk I sit typing at, there's an old Porsche advertisement. Some people might wonder why it's there. For sure, on one level it's nothing more than a catchy come-on designed to sell a few expensive German sports cars in a tough American market. And it does it by poking fun at guys like me, "car guys" who dream of finding four-wheeled treasures we never will, and couldn't afford even if we did. But here's the thing. There's something about this little snippet of capitalist catnip I like. It's got a quality I call "accidental profundity." Commercially it purports to say very little. But to guys like me who have the unfortunate habit of lusting after the very things that always elude us, it speaks volumes about the nature of our dreams.

The framed image is of the bulbous hood and front fenders of a dusty red Porsche Speedster. It's the very car I suspect Jesus Christ would insist on driving if and when he ever gets around to revisiting this sin-riddled planet. This undulating masterpiece of hand-tooled Teutonic steel is viewed through a set of open barn doors. There it sits, the car of my dreams, nesting like a hen on a bed of barn hay. The copy below it reads…

There, enshrouded in dust, sitting lopsided on a time-flattened tire, is a 1958 Porsche 356 Speedster. Left behind 25 years earlier, you discover, by a son on his way to boot camp and a subsequent commitment to marriage, family and a station wagon.

Nonchalantly, you walk around it, examining it, and realize that under the dust nothing is missing. It's all there. Waiting.

"Never got around to selling it," the old farmer who now owns the car says.

"Oh?" you reply, stifling the urge to hug a perfect stranger. "I might be interested."

"You would, eh? $500 be too much?"

And then you wake up.

Now doesn't that punch line just beat all? "And then you wake up." In a real world where dreams steadfastly refuse to come true no matter how much made-up baloney Hollywood feeds us, it seems like we're all of us just waking up at the very moment things are getting good. That little piece of hard candy truth has been breaking my teeth since I was old enough to chew. So as I tagged along behind Old Leather Gloves up his driveway, it was with zero anticipation of uncovering anything even remotely interesting in that dilapidated garage of his.

With the push of a button, a paint-deprived overhead door clattered upward with the excruciating yawn and stretch of rusty metal waking up from a long nap. Behind it lay a world of clutter where a bright, shiny family sedan might once have slumbered. Twin ceiling-to-floor walls of long-neglected lawn and garden minutia framed an alleyway down its center tight as any jungle path. With just enough room for one person moving sideways to scuffle through, I waited outside, watching as Old Leather Gloves paused to puzzle. Removing his cap, he ran long, slender fingers over his balding head. Then, reaching up, he retrieved what he'd been looking for; Pop's pipes.

Back on the drive, he handed me a round pipe rack. Each of its six cupped stations cradled a dusty briar. But it was the green onyx lid on the cut-glass humidor at its center that stopped me cold. If that jar had been the Queen of England reading a smutty men's magazine on a city bus, my eyes could not have been more riveted. I pulled it from the rack and turned it over. The yellowed but completely intact label on the bottom read ALFRED DUNHILL, LONDON, ENGLAND. Like Howard Carter brushing the last grains of sand from that first step leading down into King Tut's tomb, I tingled all over with a sense of being on the threshold of some great discovery.

My thoughts, strange as this may seem, were of my Porsche advertisement. Against all odds, for once it felt exactly like it was me standing in front of those barn doors, getting ready to feign disinterest in the find of my lifetime.

"So you say you'd like to get rid of these old pipes. Well, Old Leather Gloves, I might be interested."

Putting the humidor aside, the first pipe I slid from the rack bore a familiar white dot atop its long, elegantly tapered, grayish stem. It was a root-finished billiard easily twice the size of anything passing for a full-sized pipe these briar-starved days. On its shank, as sharp and readable as if they'd been stamped that very day, were a set of patent numbers. No doubt about it. I'd hit the motherlode. This was old wood, the stuff of pipemen's dreams.

Two of Pop's other pipes, both only marginally smaller than the first, proved to be Dunhills of the patent era as well. One, a lovely lovat with Bruyere finish and a stubby saddle bit seemed to have been a favorite smoker. Although its rim was hardly darkened, so lovingly had the whole pipe been preserved, the cake inside the bowl was thick and even as an Indian-head nickel. The other, another root finish full-bent billiard, possessed almost flawless birds-eye. Both flanks of its bowl were dark, oily kaleidoscopes of circles and swirls.

The three pipes that remained in the rack were Barlings. All were uncommonly large, possessing the florid fishtail signatures and three-digit shape numbers signaling pre-transition English pipemaking of the very highest order. Of the trio, the one that stole my eye was a dark hexagonal beauty. Its shank was banded in silver and stamped with three crisp English hallmarks and the authenticating E.B.W.B. imprint. Pop, whoever he'd been, surely was a man who knew his pipes!

Old Leather Gloves, bless his generous heart, trumped my wildest fantasy. Not content to simply offer me Pop's pipes for some ridiculously low price, he tried giving them to me for free!

"Just nice seeing this stuff finally going to a good home where it will be appreciated. Sure that's what Pop would have wanted. And I won't lie to you, son. I sure could use a little empty space in that garage."

That was my cue. In a flash I should have been in my van and gone, the treasures of my pipe-smoking lifetime rattling safely along beside me on the passenger seat. But I wasn't. To my own astonishment, I stayed to haggle. Inexplicably, I found Old Leather Gloves' insanely generous offer difficult to refuse but impossible to accept. Yes, certainly I wanted that rack and those pipes for a steal. What pipeman wouldn't? After all, that's what the dream in the Porsche ad was all about, right? But to me, standing there in that driveway with everything mysteriously going my way, suddenly it felt like there was a world of difference between getting something for a steal and stealing something outright.

I had a little over two hundred dollars in my wallet. It seemed too little to offer for pipes I knew were worth a small fortune. But it was all I had, and like I kept reminding myself, it was also two hundred dollars more than Old Leather Gloves was asking. And I damned sure wasn't gonna mush the deal by letting my moment get away. There would be no running off to a bank to get more cash. I may not be the sharpest crayon in the box, but even I know that if you're lucky enough to catch a dream by the tail, you don't dare let go.

But lack of funds proved to be the least of my problems. That's because on the other side of the negotiating table, Old Leather Gloves was finding two hundred dollars way too much to accept for something he didn't value at all. I tried convincing him that serious pipe collectors think nothing of spending thousands of dollars for someone else's dirty old pipes. But pipe collecting at the highest levels is such a private insanity, and even as I earnestly tried to make my case, the astronomical dollar amounts I bantered about sounded far-fetched even to me. Old Leather Gloves just laughed. I'm sure he thought I was making it all up.

So we began negotiating backwards toward an agreed price.

"Please," I began, "let me give you two hundred dollars. It's all that I have and far less than these pipes are worth. But if you accept it you'll make me a very happy man."

No deal. Old Leather Gloves was having none of it. As a non-pipeman, his father-in-law's old briars simply had no monetary value whatsoever. From his perspective, I suppose, accepting too large an amount of money from me would constitute stealing on his part. But perhaps sensing my urgency to give him something, he counter-offered.

"Give me fifty, son, and we'll call it a deal. How's that?"

So I gave him two fifties. I pushed both bills into his hand and he didn't so much as look down to count them. Could have been Confederate currency and I don't believe he would have cared. Just looked me in the eye and shook my hand.

"Now you be good to those old pipes, you hear me, son? The man who owned 'em before you was a fine gentleman. I honestly believe he did love those stinky old pipes. So will you promise me you'll take care of them?" And I told him I would.

And that, so help me, is exactly how the little fable foretold in my Porsche advertisement came true for me, standing right there in Old Leather Gloves' driveway. Everything was crazy and backwards and jumbled up, me, the buyer offering more, and Old Leather Gloves, the seller demanding less. In retrospect, I now see that it was all exactly as it should have been. In a word, it was dreamlike.

Mario Andretti Of Thirds

By the rules of fair marketing, a "first" is understood to be a pipe with no visible flaws in its briar or workmanship. A "second" is a pipe made by the very same pipemaker that is perceived to be of lesser quality owing to having observable shortcomings in one or both of these two vital areas. In a world where rarity rules, a "first" is the most desirable, most collectable and most expensive piece of workmanship a pipemaker is capable of producing, given the limitations of his briar and the skill in his hands. A "second" is by definition something less.

The pipe I noticed on eBay with less than two minutes of bidding to go was an observable "second" produced by the hand of a well-known pipemaker. If the sand pits and small black checks on the surface of its briar left the matter of its lowly birth in doubt, then the name stamped on the shank put those doubts to rest. Like most reputable pipe artisans, the maker of this particular pipe placed separate names on his handiwork in order to differentiate his "seconds" from his "firsts." Condemned in both name and appearance, the object of my attention was a poster child for mediocrity, an untouchable crafted in a shop of Brahmins. It was, simply put, as second as "seconds" get, and then perhaps not even that.

The reason I say this is because the pipe in question was not only heavily pre-smoked, but abused as well. A Dublin with a diamond shank and stubby bit, its silver repair band only partially hid a river of shame, a long black crack that ambled halfway up its diamond-shaped shank, a wood scar as jarring to the eye as a water snake napping on a sun-bleached log. If this pipe had been a "second" of a "first" when first fashioned, clearly, taking into consideration its now deplorable condition, it was now no better than a "second" of a "second," or, using simple pipe mathematics, a "third."

Why bid on such a pipe, you might ask. Well, I'll tell you. With two minutes to go on that hateful, relentlessly ticking down eBay clock, my mind sounded something like this. *"If this pipe were a 'first' by this maker, it would be selling for, at minimum, hundreds of dollars. If it was a perfect specimen of a 'second' it would still fetch upwards of a hundred dollars or more. And with less than two minutes to go, now less than one, NOBODY has yet to bit on it. The starting price set by the seller is fifteen dollars. And there it still sits, almost like it's invisible to everybody but me. So maybe, don't get excited now, but just maybe, for less than twenty bucks, the price for heaven's sake of dinner at the diner in this ghastly expensive age, I can purchase a handmade English pipe that might be a smoker even if it's never gonna be a looker. And look at all that tasty bird's eye. It's popping out all over the rim like brown sugar oatmeal, exactly the way great Grecian briar is suppose to look. And some lucky son-of-a-gun is gonna get it for the price of a cheeseburger platter."* And just like that, with that most unlikely image of a cheeseburger smothered in fried onions ambling around my brain, my finger tapped the "confirm" button on my computer screen. In at the speed of electronics went my last-second bid of sixteen dollars, and damned if I didn't win!

Ironically, here in America, this great land of constitutionally mandated equals, everyone wants to be first among equals. Therefore, possessing a true "first" is inordinately important to most American collectors of anything. But then there is this harsh reality. Not everyone can afford to be first or even have "firsts." Some of us, the less financially fortune graspers in the great egalitarian mob which is America, must reconcile themselves to the ownership of "seconds."

And then there are people like me. My humble home is a literal pipe hospital. My racks are littered with injured briars. Many of my most treasured pipes have cracks in their bowls. Others have cracks in the shanks. Many fail the pipe cleaner test in startling fashion. Some are drilled so high that the pipe cleaners that must be bent and mutilated to have even a snowball's chance in hell of passing into their bowls are as likely to pop out over the rim as at the base. People like me, the proprietors of pipe hospitals, are the clowns who smoke "thirds." And I'm here to tell you that every so often "thirds" really come through.

Take my latest acquisition, this squat Dublin that arrived for the price of dinner at the diner. It is an OUTRAGEOUS smoker, the best I've got. From the first puff it's been so delicious I haven't been able to put it down. I've got sixty – okay, maybe if I really counted all of them it might be closer to a hundred – pipes I smoke on a somewhat regular rotation. Between performances, some of my regulars might get a month to rest. I don't recall, until this new little pipe, ever smoking one pipe ten times in a row. But I can't help myself. And surprise, surprise, the quality of the smoke I get from this abused little workhorse just keeps getting better. Who could have guessed that such an inexpensive long-shot would turn up a winner? It's like Old Dobbins the plow horse winning the Derby or the family station wagon coming first at Indy. Yeah, and I think of my new/old little pipe in just that way, as if it were the Man-O-War of estate purchases, the Mario Andretti of "thirds."

Leg Of The Pants

One of my favorite Laurel and Hardy routines involves a pair of pants that are too long for Oliver Hardy's legs. He asks his moronic sidekick, Stan Laurel, to "shorten the legs" with a pair of scissors. Of course, being a moron, Laurel scratches his head and makes a move to shorten Hardy's actual flesh-and-blood legs with the scissor. Alarmed, Hardy exclaims, "No, no, the leg of the pants! The leg of the PANTS!"

This month, I boxed up and sent off for repair one of my problem-child pipes. It's a GBD Unique, a Horry Jamieson monstrosity in the grotesquely distorted shape of a briar calabash. Like every other GBD Unique I have ever seen, most everything about this pipe is flat-out wrong. It's always been my suspicion that Horry Jamieson was a man born to drive trucks or serve steaming hot platters of greasy diner food. But giving that man a sharp knife and a block of uncarved briar is about as insane as loaning Charlie Manson the keys to the family car and begging him to take your sister out on a date.

For one thing, the base of my potbellied briar calabash is not round. It is elongated at the heel and stained shoe polish black. Viewed from just the right angle, it has the amusing countenance of a chubby locomotive. Not much to be done about that. But this is not its only visual flaw. The extreme length of its shank and stem are way out of proportion with its bowl. It's like Horry the Horror, in a mad effort to not waste a single millimeter of raw material, just kept turning that shank till he ran clean out of plateaux briar. As a result, my GBD

185

Unique seems to have a Pinocchio nose. To be honest, if this malformed pipe wasn't a non-disposable anniversary gift from the Old Battleaxe herself, it would have been gone long ago. But it's clearly here to stay as long as the Battleaxe does.

So last month I got it in my head to try and make a bad situation better. I boxed that deformed briar of mine up and sent it off to my pipe repair guru, Mr. Jeff Walls out in Mansfield, Ohio. My written instructions to Jeff, a man who has never flinched at any of the insane things I've tasked him to do and never done me wrong in their execution, was to shorten the shank by half distance and drill a new mortise to accept the pipe's original mile-long mouthpiece. No small undertaking, but if Jeff was up to it, I figured so was I.

But for the first time ever, Jeff balked. Rather than jumping onboard for the briar cutting mayhem, he requested permission to take a baby-step before attempting a flying leap. He suggested fashioning a new, stubby mouthpiece for my GBD, a proposition that involved a tenth of the work and a fraction of the expense. The hoped for result would be the same, a more proportioned protrusion jutting from my potbellied pipe. I, of course, consented to this operation and the truncated pipe is with me now. It's still ugly as hell. Nothing can ever be done about that. It's like my sainted mom was so found of saying, "you can't make a silk purse from a sow's ear." But it is markedly better.

Looking back on this latest round of pipe repair insanity, it occurs to me that I'd offered up my pipe to Jeff and specifically requested that he "cut off the leg" (shank)" and he, very wisely, decided to cut off the "leg of the pants" (stem) instead. Clearly, when dealing with an unstable client such as myself, the role of expert pipe repairman involves more than blindly following instructions to the letter. In extreme cases such as the one described above, an expert pipe repairman such as Jeff Walls must be cognizant that pipes are not the only thing he's dealing with that's subject to breakage. A client's brain is as apt to snap as any stem, and when it does, the expert pipe repairman must recognize that human damage and say "no" to any unreasonable requests that cracked instrument might generate. Jeff Walls of Mansfield, Ohio, is just such a craftsman. I'm might fortunate to have found him.

The Father In Me

Of all the pipe stories out there, the one I enjoy hearing most is about Bo Nordh's favorite pipe. It's an oldie but goodie, and if there are more than few readers of mine who haven't already heard it, I'd be surprised. But for those unlucky few, briefly, the story goes like this. Bo Nordh, pipemaker extraordinaire, carver of multi-thousand dollar briar art forms, in short, a man who could smoke the best of the best any time he wanted, chose instead to puff on a no-name bent little pipe that looks like a cracked soup pot in a nightmarish Hieronymus Bosch painting.

The message I take away from this true little tale is this…there is no such thing as "objective value." Value as I've come to understand it is simply a measure of the things the heart wants. And because the human heart is a fickle old dog, "true value" must remain forever subjective. To remind me of this truth, I keep a picture of that little kettle-shaped pipe pinned to my corkboard right here, just above my desk.

I've sent copies of it, including its story, to my children. My hope is that these young people get the life lesson hidden in the silly note and photo from their father. Each of my kids is very much their own person. I wouldn't have it any other way. And yet, when I am alone with the father in me and secret things get whispered between us, he councils, "Your children are in some small way still your creations, and so they will get it."

Which brings me to this: each year, we, the NASPC, select a pipe to replicate and celebrate as our "Pipe of the Year." Last year it was the "Custombill," a tribute to our fallen leader, Bill Unger. In a recent submission to this newsletter, it was stated in no uncertain terms that the "Custombill" was not the most pleasing pipe to some people's eyes. It was a harshly worded judgment, one that on purely aesthetic grounds I involuntarily found myself in cahoots with. I say involuntarily because emotionally I found the article repugnant. That's because to me, there's much more to the "Custombill" than a simple pipe form. Like Bo Nordh's humble little pipe, the "Custombill" was, for those perceptive enough to receive it, a message to the heart carved in briar. It embodied the strong, good feelings I harbor for the man it was chosen to honor. To me, the subjective value in that particular "Pipe of the Year" could only be observed when looking at through the eyes of the heart. To take that particular pipe to task here in the pages of what was once Bill's newsletter on aesthetic grounds alone, no matter how honest and perhaps even accurate that assessment might have been, was to miss a much bigger point.

If the pipeman who penned "Godawfulbuttugly Pipes" was one of my children, I just know the father in me would be deeply disappointed in him. In the quiet time when secret things get said between us, he'd likely lean in and whisper, "This one, the one who wrote this brash and boastful and superficial piece, he is not one of yours. He's missed the larger point entirely." And big-time screw-up that he is, the father in me would be quite justified in saying so.

Tittering In Their Skivvies

The most puzzling response I've ever received to anything I've ever published in *The Pipe Collector* is this one-liner, sent to my home via e-mail.

"How dare you refer to your wife's brother, Dud, as a moron?"

We live in hypersensitive times. As Americans, there are things we can no longer get away with saying one to another. It often seems our prime directive as a culture is THOU SHALL NOT OFFEND. In service to that end, we've elevated the holding of our tongues to a national art form. And still, as a safety precaution against unintended misspeak, we've communally consented to the deliberate neutering of our language. To avoid dealing frankly with certain clearly observable but uncomfortable social truths, we daily alter the words we use to describe those truths. Not surprisingly, despite all our name-shifting hide-and-seek, the uncomfortable truths remain much the same. The only thing that changes is our language. Once a nifty instrument for concise communication, the English language is well on its way to becoming the stuff of code and confusion.

"Small price to pay," the political correctness czars insist, "for not offending anyone."

Now, if you've read even a single word of what ralph in jersey has published, you'll know this verbal tomfoolery is antithetical to everything he's about as a writer. As a matter of style, he offends in order to awaken the sleeping mind. So although I withhold my support from the correctness czars, I do confess to understanding where they are coming from and what they hope to accomplish by perpetrating their grammatical sleight of hand. And still, when you take into consideration the fact that Dud, the non-existent brother-in-law in question is an entirely fictional creation of mine, a made-up creature whose only reason for existence is to be moronic for comedic effect, I'm at a total loss as to how best to respond to anyone who'd ask, "How dare you refer to your wife's brother, Dud, as a moron?"

Now we all know that when you find yourself in a hole, it's best to stop digging. That just makes sense. And still, I feel strangely compelled to shovel just a bit deeper into this moron business in order to share a little something with you that you perhaps did not already know about Dud, a man whose only true defining characteristic is that he does not exist.

Let's begin with this. If Dud is understood to be a fictitious character, then his equally nonexistent daddy, Big Percy O'Sullivan, might best be described here as an equally fictitious character one generation removed. It's details that allow such made-up characters to spring to life, so just for fun, let's say Big Percy was conscripted into the U.S. Army during the final, dangerous days of World War II. When asked for their best recollection, both of Big Percy's nonexistent children, my wife, the Old Battleaxe herself, and her baby brother, Dud, seem to think Big Percy received his infantry training at a now long defunct fort somewhere in the Deep South. The wife insists it was somewhere in Texas. When Dud can be bothered to think at all, he's rather inclined to believe it was more likely in Louisiana or Alabama. But wherever it was, it was there, at this geographically nebulous fort that Big Percy learned to fire a carbine, lob grenades and stab at straw dummies with a pointy bayonet. But because he possessed the luck of the Irish and could type about as well as any man in uniform, as deadly bullets flew on the Continent, Big Percy found himself safely ensconced behind a desk at Allied command headquarters in England.

Even that was no bed of roses. After all, the Blitz was on. Herr Hitler's Luftwaffe was up to serious no good. Nazi bombs were falling like rabbit poop all over London. Brits everywhere were being forced to live the lives of gentrified moles, hunkering down for the better parts of their days in air-raid shelters and drafty, smelly underground railroad stations. But not Big Percy. A lover of smoking pipes and long ambling strolls, the subterranean life was not for my fictitious father-in-law. Whilst centuries-old landmarks were being reduced to rubble all around him and block-long fires raged, he bravely strode the chaotic streets of London, a beloved briar cupped in his steady hand. The ear-piecing screech of Herr Hitler's beloved Stuka dive bombers held no terror for Big Percy O'Sullivan.

Befitting a man imbued with the luck of the Irish, on the very night one of those German bombs finally hit the jackpot, crashing down through the soot-blackened roof of the Dunhill store on Jermyn Street and three floors of immaculately polished glass showcases and slumbering pipes to explode with a deafening kaboom against the cold concrete of a basement floor, the compression propelling pipes and broken china out in an ear-popping whoosh onto the surrounding pavement, Big Percy O'Sullivan just happened to be passing by. Bobbies in chin-strapped helmets blew shrill whistles. The glow from burning buildings transformed night into day. And in the flickering crimson of that false, hot dawn, all around his feet, scattered like discarded seeds beneath a messy bird feeder, Big Percy beheld white-dotted pipes.

Among the precious pipes that took that most violent flight from velvet to cobblestone in the flash of an explosive moment was a treasure trove of some of the most irreplaceable Dunhills ever crafted. The best of the best were blown directly out of Old Alf Dunhill's own personal collection. Exactly how many of those museum-grade beauties landed up in Big Percy's pockets will never be known. But for sure there were lots.

A year later, most of those white-dotted gems arrived unceremoniously in the United States, jumbled up amidst unwashed socks and rank underwear at the bottom of Big Percy's duffle bag. Sadly, a few were lost in transit in an all-night card game held in the bowels of a homeward bound troop transport ship. Inexplicably, for once, the luck of the Irish seems to have deserted my fictitious father-in-law to be. His aces up two pair got themselves trounced by a big-mouthed platoon sergeant's three deuces. A grossly overweight cigar chewer who didn't know a Dunhill ODC from a drugstore corncob, the sweaty Sarge raked in his pot of two gigantic straight-grained pipes and a crumpled pile of small bills with a single grunt of purest indifference.

The cards were running badly for Big Percy that night. Out of cash and with lots more pipes still to lose, the evening was in real danger of ending up a pipe history disaster. Mercifully, a baby-faced private who hadn't won a hand all night suggested right then might be as good a time as any to hit the hay. The cards were put up for the night. Big Percy's remaining pipes were saved…for the time being.

As kids, Dud and the wife remember those gigantic Dunhills with all their confusing stampings and silver trappings collecting dust in two, three-tiered racks in their father's den. Another dozen or so sat like leather clams in their fitted cases along an empty bookshelf behind Big Percy's desk. They say war changes men. That was certainly true of Big Percy.

When the Germans surrendered to the Allies, he came home to surrender himself to his real first love, heavy drinking. For you see, as so often happens, the luck of the Irish had come at a price. Along with the luck of the Leprechauns, Big Percy inherited the notorious Irish thirst as well. A two-fisted public drinking man if ever there was one, briar pipes and all the bulky accoutrements they necessitated did not lend themselves to his new life as a barfly. In short order, the pipes that had been his faithful companions throughout the war were replaced by less cumbersome Camel cigarettes and a Zippo lighter.

Ike was still President when Momma Rose, Big Percy's long-suffering bride, had him committed to his first V.A. detox center. While Kennedy faced down Khrushchev over missiles in Cuba, Big Percy was facing down an operation to have his destroyed liver replaced. And just about the same time Richard Nixon lifted off from the White House lawn in Marine One, never again to occupy the Oval Office he'd so thoroughly disgraced, Big Percy lifted off for the afterlife, dead of lung cancer at age fifty-three.

Momma Rose got the house, the car and the life insurance. Within two years she'd shed seventy pounds, dyed and re-styled her hair, learned country line dancing and remarried. The lucky man, Mel Slotnick, purportedly wore cowboy boots to bed. Good for her, I say! But sadly, in her euphoric rush to begin the much deserved second act of her life, inexplicably, in one of the great travesties of made-up O'Sullivan family history, Momma Rose allowed her son, Dud, to get his moronic hands on those Dunhill pipes.

If you truly love pipes and don't handle loss and pain well, now might be as good a time as any to stop reading. Remember, my intention in fabricating these unpleasant family happenings has been to make my best case for calling my worthless brother-in-law, Dud, anything I damn well please, even in politically sensitive times. I therefore have no intention of candy-coating what's to follow.

Like two small storms pouring into each other to create one larger perfect storm, about the same time my mother-in-law was making herself over and hopping into the hay with her Jewish cowboy, Dud began keeping regular company with a mindless vixen who went about town calling herself "Ginger." This despite the fact that everyone in the small community in which we'd all grown up knew perfectly well that her real name was Estelle Fox, and that she was undoubtedly the town slut.

It was Ginger/Estelle who first introduced Dud to pot. It was Ginger/Estelle who convinced him that things they could easily steal from his mother's house could be converted into cash, which could then be used to buy pot they could enjoy together. A big part of that enjoyment, at least as far as Dud was concerned, was smoking his brains out and having animal sex with Ginger/Estelle in the cramped back seat of his Chevrolet station wagon. During this sad period, my wife recalls Dud coming home at all hours completely disheveled, shirt pulled out of his pants, fly open, reeking of pot, a stupid smile plastered all over his moronic face.

Within a few months the china, the silverware, and yes, all those Dunhill pipes were gone, sold for chump change or little plastic bags half-filled with twigs and leaves into the uncaring hands of depraved, nameless, faceless drug pushers. Priceless, irreplaceable pipes gone, lost, pissed away forever in return for junkie fixes that most nights lasted no longer than Dud's pathetic erection. Now, hearing this, knowing this, is there a single pipeman out there who wants to defend my brother-in-law as being anything other than a complete moron? I thought not!

Oh, and how's this for a jaw-dropping postscript? Two of Big Percy's wartime Dunhills remain in my personal collection to this day. One is a gigantic bulldog the size of a prizefighter's fist, the biggest Dunhill of that shape I've ever seen. The other is a Root-finished lumberman with a wide, flattened oval shank. End-to-end it measures over ten inches long, with an elegant thin-walled bowl almost three inches tall. It's a behemoth of a pipe embellished with a hallmarked silver band as gaudy as a circus horse's collar.

Like prisoners in a death camp that manage to survive by proving themselves useful in some way to their captors, these two extraordinary survivor pipes share a similar history. It was pot that put them in jeopardy in the first place, and ironically, it was pot that was the means of their survival. Even as their brother and sister pipes were being traded off into the uncaring hands of drug pushers who lacked all understanding of their intrinsic value and therefore gave no care for their preservation and protection, the two survivor pipes remained firmly in family possession. They did so because my moronic future brother-in-law, Dud, and his drug/sex princess, Ginger/Estelle, needed one or two pipes in which to smoke their contraband.

I challenge you to think about that one for a few moments, my fellow pipe puffers. Consider, as I have had to consider all these years, the image of Dud and his dope-addled sex goddess tittering in their skivvies as they jam sticky, smelly hashish and pot into the virgin bowls of two of the most perfect Dunhill pipes ever created. Try envisioning that depraved scene without the word "moron" popping into your mildly nicotine-addicted minds.

What I Deserved

Stopped by my old tobacco shop, the one I managed in what now seems another, much younger lifetime. Against all odds, the plush red carpet still covers the floor and the glass cases are as shiny as ever. Only thing missing were the pipes.

Back in my day – that would be the Sixties for the decade curious among you - we displayed over three hundred pipes in those cases and on the felt-lined wall racks behind them. All gone now. Cigars, cigars, cigars…that's all that remains. The little chess table by the window has been swapped out for a behemoth television the size of a highway billboard. No more jazz playing softly through the nappy beige grills of my AR-2 speakers. Gone are my soft-spoken regulars debating Fischer/ Spassky and Ali/Frasier, transformed in a slag heap of time into a couple of overweight stogie chewers, catatonic gargoyles staring silent and dead-eyed at a meaningless football contest.

The only meaningful connection to the shop's honorable past as a real "tobacco shop" is a six-pipe rack of dusty estate briars. I ask the cigar-smoking clerk, a sullen middle-aged man with nicotine-stained whiskers, if I might "get a closer look at that full-bent pipe on the end." "Sure," he says. And then, as he's struggling to get at that long overlooked pipe with its little white spot, he adds, trying to be helpful, I suppose, "I think this one might actually be a Dunhill. Dunhills were once a very high end Italian pipe, you know."

A serious factual blunder for a man in his line of work, I think we might all agree. But I don't blame the clerk. Really, his only crime, if crime it be, is that he's obviously a cigar guy of below average intelligence trying to earn his way as a clerk in a joint calling itself a tobacco shop but that's really a cigar lounge. Nothing criminal about that. No, the way I see it, I'd probably gotten just about what an old pipe guy deserves for snooping too deeply into his long-gone past.

Wimp On A Hobo's Budget

I consider Rich Esserman to be one of the most informed and informing contributors to the Pipe Collector. And yet, to date, I don't believe I've ever quite managed to get all the way through one of his epic reports. God knows, that's not for lack of content. Rich Esserman packs more pipe info into one paragraph than the rest of us wrestle into an entire article. No. I think my inability to go the distance with Rich's marathon journalism speaks more to the breath of our hobby than any shortcoming in his writing. I mean, pipe collecting and smoking is a "big tent" hobby. All you need do to gain entrance into the Big Top is love pipes. But some of us love smoking humble cobs, while others lay out big bucks for unsmoked "art pipes." Within our hobby there is ample room for similarities and differences.

I think Rich Esserman, owing to his niche interest in rare briars the size of softballs, speaks to a segment of our broad brotherhood to which I am not privy. What briars I've managed to accrue are puny by comparison. I am a self-confessed smoking wimp on a hobo's budget. Why, if I was to show up at one of those pre-pipe show smoking suites that Rich Esserman frequents and attempt to match him puff-for-puff with one of his own pipes, they'd find me dead of a nicotine overdose in that very same suite the next morning. I rate my pipe manhood as being no bigger than Group 4 tops. Give me a half-hour's worth of frantic puffing on a fifty dollar eBay estate pipe (I smoke as I eat and love…too damn fast) and I'm done, finished, kaput. So as much as I admire Rich Esserman for his meandering erudition, much of what he says in the Pipe Collector misses my mark.

Anyway, that was true up till this last edition, when Rich quoted Franco Coppo, the famous 'Kino' of Castello pipes. *"A pipe is only a more-or-less pleasing inanimate piece of wood until it is has taken on that warm colour that comes from being well-smoked: only at that point, when its reactions to tobacco combustion in its bowl have been revealed, does it become a real pipe…"* Have you ever known something but never heard it codified in words? That happens to me all the time. Sometimes I'll even say it myself in something I'm writing. I'll be clattering along, and suddenly have to take my hands off the keyboard and gaze at the words on my page and say out loud, "Damn, I always knew that. I just didn't know I knew it till just now."

Well, when Rich Esserman quoted Kino Coppo in what otherwise remains another partially unread piece of his first-rate journalism, for me it was one of those clarifying moments, and it got me to thinking this. If there was a make-believe church where all pipe smokers went to pray, over the door of that church should and would be chisel in stone the words of Kino Coppo. *"only at that point, when its reactions to tobacco combustion in its bowl have been revealed, does it become a real pipe."*

Taking A Pass

Rich Esserman, in his recent report on the 2014 New York Pipe Show, notes that "ralph in jersey stopped by to say hello." Sadly, I'm here to tell Rich he's been hacked, bamboozled, maybe even made the brunt of somebody's little joke. I say this because I, the real, the one-and-only ralph in jersey, took a pass on this year's New York Pipe Extravaganza. If it's any consolation to Rich, he should know that he is not alone in falling for this scam. There has been a contagion of ralph in jersey imitators of late, a veritable circus clown car full of them. They seem to be everywhere. Why, just last night I stopped by my local liquor emporium to pick up a medicinal bottle of Chivas Regal, and was told by the proprietor, my old pal Charlie Trout, that he was surprised to "see me again." When I asked Charlie what he meant by this, he told me I'd been in minutes before to pick up a bottle of the very same "medicine," which of course I hadn't. Whether all this masquerading and identity theft business is the result of all my newfound fame, my book, DOCTOR OF PIPES selling like hotcakes as a result of my half-page ad in the April edition of the Pipe Collector, I just don't know. But if this is what it feels like to be a rock star, or for that matter the grand champion of Bowling for Dollars, ralph in jersey would just a soon take another pass.

Fast And Loose With The Truth

Okay, ralph in jersey plays fast and loose with the truth. He's even been known to play fast and loose with the spirit of the truth. Anyone who knows the man will tell you he is intellectually lazy. He researches nothing. If an interesting disarrangement of letters in a misspelled word pleases his eye, he refuses to change it. Even so, when it's pointed out to him in print that in one of his pseudo-journalistic forays he's somehow cross-pollinated the actual first names of two famous Union generals, Phillip Sheridan and William Tecumseh Sherman, and in so doing created a Union general of his own making, a totally non-existent fellow named General Phillip Sherman, ralph in jersey knows he's deserving of a good writerly beating.

But being scolded by a coven of Civil War eggheads from New York of all places *(Who even knew there were Civil War eggheads in places like Huntington, Long Island? Not me!)* about how General Nathan Bedford Forest never campaigned outside the deep South, that right there is a bridge too far and a camelback-breaking straw if ever there was one. In my utterly tongue-in-cheek screed in the October PIPE COLLECTOR entitled STUB OF ITSELF, in an attempt to generate some real Rebel enthusiasm for a faux campaign to savagely over-light smoking pipes, I'd invited any and all Dixie sympathizers to fantasize that General Nathan Bedford Forest, heroic Southern raider and dark-minded father of the Ku Klux Klan, was sacking the Yankee capital at Washington, D.C. Fantasize. Fantasize. Fantasize.

I think pipemen as a group, for better and for worse, tend to ponder and plod more than most. Make the smallest factual error in a pipe journal that's being pawed over by a pack of eagle-eyed pipe puffers professing a briar kinship with Sherlock Holmes, and you better expect to get caught. But damn, my brothers, what has happened to our ability to separate fact from fiction? Fantasy, as I've always understood it, is the freeform art of throwing facts to the wind and watching them scatter for the shear joy of doing it. At the risk of appearing an alarmist, I'm going to suggest certain select pipemen hailing from a thin sliver of historically insignificant land protruding upward out of the sack-like enclave of New York City, a water-bound snot of swampy marshland that on a map looks for all the world like, well, let's just say it looks like a pinky sticking up from a fist, might be losing the fine balance between the bad of plod and good of ponder.

So tonight I challenge all pipemen everywhere to don your beloved deerstalkers and lift your precious pipes to all those nicotine-tinged lips and ponder this…what does it say about us as a strange tribe of briar-obsessed lunatics when we begin presuming to fact-check one another's fantasies?

Mysterious Sacrament Of Confiscation

I suppose it's no secret by now that ralph in jersey likes his old pipes "oily." By this he means briars that somehow find a way to shine even though they are very obviously dull, the lucky, magical few whose glow seems to originate beneath the surface of their wood, almost as though the grain was being back-lit by some inner light.

As luck would have it, I'm smoking just such a pipe right now. It's an old veteran of the smoking wars, a brown as a nut GBD Century. That "rub-off" Century finish with its confounding ability to go from morning wheat to midnight coffee in a smoke or two has always been one of my very favorites. This old taper-stemmed pot, after years of repeated firings, literally glows with a subdued luster that for me defines pipe beauty.

And like all spectacular things that command my attention and demand my admiration, looking down into this great dark pool of a pipe has set my mind to wondering. The thought that's come is this…we foolish mortals enjoy tricking ourselves into believing that true beauty is a docile creature capable of being corralled into gaudy frames on museum walls. But lucky for all of us, true beauty is a wild thing. Velvet ropes and golden stanchions can't contain it. It goes where it pleases and does what it will.

If you know how to look, wild beauty might be encountered in the simple act of waking up. For those fortunate enough to not be sleeping alone, it can greet us straightaway in the drowsy smile of a special friend. For others it might be there in things as mundane as sunshine on the ceiling, wind at the window or sun-flecked ripples on a lake. But it is there. All we need is eyes to see it.

And often just seeing it is enough. I suppose that's why we have all those gilded frames in all those carefully roped off echoy museums. A day spent gazing at extraordinary beauty can lift our spirits and energize our imaginations. And that's no small joy. But beauty is a playful thing. At the very best of times, she allows us to interact with her.

Take those ripples on that lake at the bottom of this mountain I call home. Every day, depending on the mood of the sun and the whimsy of the clouds, as I stop to look both ways before turning my car or motorcycle in the direction of dreaded work, that great natural bathtub of glistening water greets me. Each and every day it's a changeable feast for my eyes.

But for those with boats with sails and strong hands to grip a tiller, it is more still. Those lucky sailors tack and glide, and at the end of their dizzying day on the water, sails furled and ropes tied fast, they take that diamond-eyed chop on the lake home with them not only as a reflection in their eyes, but in the memories of their tired muscles. Those who are able to make that physical connection with beauty, they are the double-lucky few.

And we pipemen can count ourselves among their ranks. Through our beloved pipes we too are able to possess beauty in the same measure as those sailors. We select a pipe from our rack to smoke. We hold it in our hand and admire it, the color, the shape, the artful dots and swirls imprinted in the wood that never grow tiresome. And that is enough. And then there is more. Because our pipes are more than just beautiful.

They are playful as well. They use their beauty to lure us into interaction with them in exactly the same way water and wind lures the sailor. The very best pipes are temptresses possessing all the guile of a woman on fire seducing her lover. And so, helpless to resist, like a pathetic pack of moon-eyed love slaves we pack our briars with tobacco and strike our kitchen matches. And if we are both attentive and receptive, through the flavor of their smoke the essence of our pipes flows into us.

It is an intimate ritual we perform. It is an act of possession in a way that few other things are. And make no mistake. Such up-close-and-personal dalliances with true beauty are a very great human joy. There is a magic to them that those who've experienced it will tell you it does more than simply lift spirits and energize imaginations. Because intimate interaction with true beauty has a way of tricking us into believing we are more beautiful ourselves.

Don't believe me? Just ask the very next lecherous old codger you spy with his pathetically flabby arm wrapped around the waist of a drop-dead gorgeous young woman how it feels to possess true beauty. Notice the adolescent twinkle in the horny old satyr's eyes as he tells you all about it. Those eyes will tell you all you need to know about the act of confiscating beauty.

Or easier still, ask the very next way over-the hill pipeman you encounter who looks like he belongs in a nursing home but is dressed up like he's going on a fox hunt about the mystically invigorating properties of that outrageously beautiful pipe he's got clenched between his hideously yellowed teeth. If he is a forthcoming sort of chap, and most pipemen are, chances are he'll know all about this mysterious sacrament of confiscation that only occurs when true beauty is totally possessed. Yes, if the old fool is smoking his pipe the same way I smoke mine, he'll have no problem telling you all about it.

Pretty But Unpleasant Reminders

Money in exchange for things is always a tricky proposition. To illustrate that point, let me tell you a little story about what happened after my mother died. Greedy capitalist family that we are, we decided to have a house sale. It was scheduled to kick off at nine in the morning. An hour before, the line of milling strangers on mom's walk stretched clear down into the street. When the clock struck the appointed hour, in they trampled. Seven hectic hours later we'd exchanged a house full of family heirlooms for a shopping bag crammed with cash. Crinkled bills loosely fluffed can look like a fortune. So as we tidied up, I think it fair to say we were all pretty pleased with both ourselves and the day's haul.

By way of celebration, everyone who'd lent a hand headed out to get a bite to eat. Wine, pasta, espresso, even gooey dessert for a few ladies whose waistlines could easily have done without gooey dessert. Three glutinous hours later our bag of loot was gone.

That night as I tossed in bed trying to sleep, I realized all I was going to take away from my madhouse day at mom's was the ugly memory of a surging mob of impolite strangers tracking callously through the house that had sheltered me since childhood. They pulled things down, opened closets and drawers, all the while haggling endlessly as if their cheap-ass lives depended on negotiating the absolute lowest price for every blessed trinket they could lay their greedy mitts on.

What little sleep I got that night was not restful. I awoke knowing I'd paid a heavy price for my stupidity. But if a black cloud has no silver lining, I can be depended upon to fabricate one. What I convinced myself I'd gotten in compensation from my fiasco was an expensive but invaluable lesson in the unwise exchange of money for things.

I haven't done much selling since. Not of things that matter anyway. As a result, my home is a den of clutter. But I'm not complaining. The way I see it, clutter is simply the price one pays for being unwilling to pay the price for cleaning up. It's the same zero sum game we all play with ourselves over everything we do in this life. Whether we notice it or not, as new things arrive in our lives, it is most always at the expense of something of equal but opposite value departing. Yes, it's a mysteriously balanced world we inhabit. I've made my peace with that.

So it came as a bit of a surprise to me when recently, after years of acquiring estate pipes on eBay, I finally got around to parting with a few. And not just any few, because by any objective standard, the pipes I've jettisoned are among the very best I owned. For you see, most of the used pipes I pluck from the eBay cyber-ether are refugees from somebody else's trash heap. My average used briar purchase puts me back somewhere between thirty and seventy-five dollars. I pride myself on thinking that if you have an eye for "good wood," then you can get yourself some startlingly fine smoking pipes slumming in such low rent retail neighborhoods. I know I have.

But every so often I allow myself to wander off my own financial reservation. The thought that precedes all such unwise forays is always the same. The Little Troublemaker in my brain whispers, "If you're getting this much pleasure out of these el cheapo pipes, then perhaps someone else who's spending twice as much for his is getting double your pleasure."

Thank god there is a Wise Council in my brain as well. And such misleading and potentially damaging subliminal messages from the Little Troublemaker always catch their attention. Alarms sound. An emergency session of the Wise Council is convened. It is invariably decreed that the Little Troublemaker is to be ignored at all cost. But the Little Troublemaker is amazingly strong and frightfully persistent for someone so diminutive in size. And to be perfectly frank, even though the members of the Wise Council are unquestionably sagacious in the extreme, when it comes to laying down the law they can be a pathetic pack of mealy-mouthed cowards. So quite predictably, eventually an expensive "mistake pipe" appears in my mailbox.

These expensive-for-me pipes always fail to satisfy. They are simply outside my comfort zone. It's not that they don't smoke at least as well as my hobo pipes. Some actually do, although it might be important to note that thus far none have smoked any better. And left with a choice between two briars that to my undiscerning taste smoke identically, one an unassuming English shape of Group 4 proportion, the other an ostentatious piece of briar puffery befitting the jaw of a monarch, invariably, being a man of pedestrian sensibilities, I reach for the hobo every time.

Like those little creamer pods that diner waitresses insist on bombarding your table with whenever coffee is ordered, these mistake pipes just sit around creating clutter. They are financial travesties from the get-go. But I'm never satisfied poking out just one of my financial eyes, For me, a good self-blinding requires the poking out of both eyes. This I accomplish by purchasing, for no reason I can justify or explain, an expensive pipe holder for each and every one of my misfit pipes. A brass

Scotty dog here, a tiger or supine ceramic sailorman there; I assure you, it all adds up. And in the end, these exorbitant host pipes and the strange and unwanted suck-fish holders they attract land up as unsmoked decorations in a cabin cluttered to claustrophobia with other such oddities.

They make swell curios, these mistake pipes, but as smoking instruments they simply don't make the grade. That mysterious bonding all collectors of estate pipes are intimately familiar with, the process by which someone else's grimy old pipe suddenly and irrevocably becomes one's own, well, that never happens between me and my expensive mistake pipes. I perform all the rituals prerequisite to making it happen. I clean them. I rub them. I smoke them. I wait for the magical transference to occur. I wait for them to become mine and it does not happen.

So perhaps not surprisingly, I recently parted with a few such misfits. One was a horn-shaped Savinelli Autograph, the only pipe in my collection regal enough to be crowned with bumpy plateau grain. This jewel of the Italian pipemaker's art even arrived and departed tied in rawhide and swaddled in its very own calf-skin pouch. I purchased that piece of royal briar just out of college. I'm sixty-seven now, and if I was to say I smoked that pipe two dozen times in a half-a-century, that would be an exaggeration.

Now I have nothing against Italian pipemakers, you understand. Okay, maybe Italians do make beautiful but mechanically junky automobiles. And yes, I once spent two fortunes on a pair of glove-soft leather wing-tipped shoes from the boot-shaped land of pasta and pizza that were the color of a newborn calf's backside. And those shoes fell apart the first time I wore them in the rain. But Italians make tasty pipes. I have several I smoke all the time. Both are relatively inexpensive and of modest proportion. One, a Linea 76, a thick-walled, limited edition pipe sold for one year only to mark the company's one-hundredth year of pipemaking, is one of my very best smokers. So why didn't I ever pick up the Autograph? It was, simply put, just too damned grand.

Another pipe that's gone is a Castello full-bent "egg" Easily twice the size of my next largest pipe, its flanks are a master painter's canvas of birds-eye to die for. It arrived here several years ago, the physical manifestation of a mad directive that seemed to fall directly from the sky into my head. From out of nowhere I received this garbled transmission. "If you are to own a Castello," the alien voice in my head commanded despite the fact that I did not want to own one, "then let it be a grand one!" And thus, inevitably as day follows night, when it arrived unwanted, a very grand one it was. Grander than anything I'd ever dreamed of owning or even wanting to own by a mile.

It all made about as much sense to me as a hundred dollar a day cleaning lady saving all her earnings to purchase a diamond tiara. And just as it figures that the tiara isn't going to get out of its felt-lined case for want of an occasion grand enough to justify wearing it, my grand Castello full-bent "egg" seldom got up from its pipe holder. For the Queen of England or the Sultan of Swat, my Castello would have been perfect. But for a whiskery old recluse living in a forest, it was flat out too gaudy. No special occasion circled on my Norman Rockwell calendar could ever justify the smoking of such a spectacle pipe in public. And even in the privacy of my home, having that Mardi Gras of a pipe stuck between my teeth made me feel like a circus clown.

So both pipes are gone now, exchanged for what passes for currency out on the Internet. For the first time in all my years of doing business with them, my eBay account shows a positive balance. Something lost and something gained, it's that old zero balance world at play again. And in the interest of full disclosure and accurate accounting, I should confess that positive account balance is shrinking faster than Al Roker's waistline. If you've ever had such a precarious positive balance sitting just one easy "click" away from being effortlessly reconverted into some new frivolous purchase, then I don't have to tell you that all eBay balances are by design not meant to last.

The morning after my mistake pipes sold, that balance peaked at just over six hundred dollars. This month's e-statement shows me still in possession of approximately half those funds. Now I do remember purchasing a few replacement pieces for the wife's china serving. There was also for sure a chunk of cash sent off to a "Canadian pharmacy" somewhere in India for a packet of generic blue pills that somehow manage to keep my penis serviceable in a love tussle. And oh yes, fifty dollars was sent off with my blessings to West Texas to purchase a small but nifty piece of art from my very talented and very eclectic niece. No regrets there.

But do those recalled acquisitions account for the whole of my missing three hundred dollars? Not nearly. But to have a positive eBay account balance to is like having a slow leak in a car tire. I know that. And mounting a fool's errand to account for exactly where every last pound/penny of your air/cash has gone will only make you crazy. Money is to the workingman in America what dirt is to the earthworm. It is a totally transient substance that goes in at the front and exits at the rear. It is the stranger who knocks on our door but never stays long enough to visit.

So yes, I confess, in the end I will knowingly have exchanged my two spectacular pipes for a meaningless eBay account balance that by its very nature was always intended to disappear. You might be thinking it's that old exchanging money for things scam that caught me out at mom's place all those years ago. And you might even be thinking, "Hey, this chucklehead has learned nothing. Fifty years later and he's still making the same stupid mistake!"

But you'd be wrong, because I have learned something. For you see, after the fiasco of the house sale, what I was left with once the crinkled money in the bag evaporated was a slew of bad memories of strangers defiling mom's house. With the pipes, again the money will soon be gone with nothing particularly tangible to take its place. But this time I have gotten something intangible for my troubles.

That's because having pipes I'm not comfortable with sitting around my house sets off a low voltage alarm signal in my head that I just can't shut off. And let me tell you something. Mental static like that, no person should have to live with. Mistake pipes are pretty but unpleasant reminders that the better angels of our nature don't always have the upper hand. "Yes," these little briar monuments remind me, "you are a person who is smart enough to know better, but at the same time you are a person who is too dumb to do anything about it. You can't help acting stupidly despite how smart you are, and the worst part is you're just clever enough to have to watch yourself doing it!" And who wants to be continually reminded of that day after day within the confines of one's own home?

So money be damned. What I have to show for selling those two mistake pipes does not show up on any bank statement or ledger sheet. But "so what" I say! Peace of mind doesn't jingle like loose change in your pocket. It's not furry like a rabbit's foot you can reach down and stroke. Peace of mind is more like running a fever. When you've got a good high one going, you sure as hell don't need any rinky-dink thermometer or broken down old sawbones to tell you the score.

And as if that were not enough, there is this added bonus too. Just knowing that out there somewhere there is somebody with an ego big enough to go toe-to-toe with those twin circus pipes of mine has put a gigantic, bemused smile on my kisser that just won't wipe off. Now just try putting a price tag on something as priceless as that!

Woman With Two Tongues

Addressing himself to pornography, a jurist whose name I cannot recall famously said, "I may not be able to tell you what it is, but I damn well know it when I see it." I think presuming to know exactly how many pipes constitute "enough" for any particular collector lands us in this very same thorny briar patch. As pipe smokers and collectors, one day we're buying and selling and swapping like a pack of Ecstasy-crazed swingers at the Playboy Mansion. The next day, for no reason we can fathom, a mental buzzer goes off inside our pipe collector heads and, just like that, it's game over. We've had enough. Our collections seem strangely complete. And although, yes, old habits do die hard and we can still look and even occasionally buy a stray pipe, the compulsion is gone. Yes, we still can, but no, we don't have to.

The change I'm describing is subtle, but its arrival can feel profound indeed. It is, I suppose, analogous in many ways to the human sex drive. When we're young and awash in bothersome hormones, impure thoughts of the opposite sex can be all-consuming. By middle age, for better and for worse, the sexual mental static begins to abate. And if, again, for better and for worse we live long enough to find ourselves old and decrepit, that rascally old compulsion that resides just below our belts becomes almost a take-it-or-leave-it affair. Yeah, sure, sex is still a hoot when it happens, but we no longer find ourselves barhopping half the night making public fools of ourselves in order to make sure it does.

I think the change that comes over pipe collectors can be just like that. Anyway, I know it was for me. My pipe racks and rests, once literal beehives of new comings and old goings, seem eerily stable these days. When I stroll around the house inventorying my pipes, as I often do, I feel strangely like a parent who's survived the chaos of raising a large family and who can not now, for love or money, conceive of having or wanting any more children. Oh sure, I still find myself leering at suggestive photos of sexy pipes on eBay. On any given evening I might see one or two dark, oily briars I'd love to caress with my hot little hands. But these days I do ninety-nine percent of all my caressing with my eyes and my wallet stays closed.

Old analogies die hard. So again I'll confess a kinship to the old codger sitting on a park bench ogling lovely young ladies as they sashay by. But like the codger, as a pipeman I no longer come to my collector's bench to possess the objects of my affection. My finger no longer twitches with nervous anticipation over the BID button as that infuriating eBay clock ticks its way down to zero. These days I come to simply watch and appreciate, and yes, if the opportunity presents itself, perhaps feed a pigeon or two.

So after almost two years on the eBay sidelines, last week it felt like quite an event when I at last did get myself back in the old purchasing game. I couldn't resist this one. A history buff since grammar school, for me, certain dates possess historical gravitas that others lack. For instance, 1776 and 1917 are BIG years. 1777 and 1916 pale in comparison. So while dating is not the first thing I consider when purchasing a pipe, if a briar I'm already liking for other, saner, more easily explained reasons happens to be silver hallmarked or stamp-coded for some year I consider BIG, then all the better.

And for me personally, 1947 is as BIG as they come. It's my birth year. I've always had my eye out – figuratively, of course – for a nice briar that was being manhandled atop some obscure craftsman's workbench at the very moment I was busy being born. This new pipe, my "late-in-life child" as it were, is a straight Peterson billiard with a silver band bearing the hallmark of my birth year. It's a great old piece of dull, dignified briar.

Only thing I hold against it is this. Through no fault of its own, it was created with a dopey Peterson P-lip, that ridiculous extra dollop of vulcanite squished onto the behind of the button exactly like as if it were the miniaturized hump of a tiny sperm whale, its blow hole poking foolishly upward. I hate P-lips. I've never learned what to do with them when they are in my mouth. It always seems my tongue or some other saliva-drenched piece of personal anatomy is partially obstructing that weirdly aimed smoking spout. To me, smoking a Peterson pipe with a P-lip feels as unnatural as French-kissing a woman with two tongues. And I blame myself for that. Like the backhoe operator too stupid to find the slot for the ignition key, I seem to lack the innate intelligence necessary to operate a piece of smoking machinery as complex as the Peterson P-lip.

But not one to be easily deterred, I contacted a number of Briar Brotherhood luminaries by e-mail, soliciting their sage advice on how I might best proceed. They responded as if with one mind. All counseled that I not modify the existing stem. All confessed no love of the P-lip. And still, there was a uniformity of opinion that the unwieldy lump of rubber protruding from the smoking end of my 1947 birthday pipe's stem, monstrous blot against the pipemaker's art that it is, should be treated as a sacrosanct malignancy, a growth not to be excised.

As I researched the matter, it became quite clear to me that there are higher laws governing pipe modifications, and these laws are in no way ambiguous. The applicable legal precedent governing the matter of P-lips states that if a stem is created with a pipe, it should, in all cases not involving the health and welfare of the pipe itself, remain unaltered and with that pipe. This was the unanimous declaration of the Council of the Wise. To take a file to an original Peterson P-lip would be the pipe equivalent of removing the bulbous front bumper from a 1950 Studebaker and replacing it with the sleeker and more eye-catching chrome hardware from a 1956 Corvette. A visual upgrade for sure, but an automotive design travesty to boot.

Now I've got another confession to make. For those who may not have already guessed, let me make one thing perfectly clear. I am an odd duck. Quick to seek sage advice, I'm slow to take it. So against advice of council, I got out my trusty pipe mutilation kit. Five minutes with a flat file and that offensive blob of vulcanite behind the button that separates P-lips from all other pipes that smoke properly was but a memory, a design travesty reduced to a pile of black shavings on the floor around my feet. Ever wonder where that ridiculous skyward-pointing smoke tunnel goes, how and where it turns to join the main smoke channel and what the back of such a Peterson stem would look like if that obscene lump of unnecessary rubber was well and properly guillotined? Well, I'm here to tell you.

Predictably, with all but about an eighth of an inch of material filed away from behind the sharp front rim of the button, that silly bit of vertical nonsense is already fully horizontal, passing into the now conventional flat back end of the button at its very top. What is surprising is how shockingly narrow its circumference is. If Rick Newcombe or any other hardcore advocate for fully opened pipe airways were to see it, they'd fall to their knees and proceed to poke their eyes out with a three-way Czechoslovakian pipe pick in horror.

All my P-lipped Peterson pipes have been gurglers. And when they gurgle, just try jamming a pipe cleaner down inside them to mop up the soggy goop. Good luck with that! Easier, I think, for jolly old St. Nick to squeeze his jelly belly down a chimney flue. 'Cause there at the very end, right where it once made its smoke-constricting corkscrew turn down into the stem itself, the hole in my birthday Peterson's stem was about the width of a straightened paper clip wire. Why so narrow? Maybe it has something to do with the geometry of drilling and turning that subatomic aperture in such a constricted radius. A less kind interpretation might seek fault with those tall pints of dark beer all those lusty Irishmen at the Peterson factory figure to be swilling down with their pickled luncheon meats. But whatever its genealogy, that pleasure killing constriction undoubtedly accounts for most of the wheezing and gurgling one is likely to encounter with a P-lipped Peterson.

A hard dose of truth, I'm sure, for Peterson pipe lovers to wolf down. But again I would emphasize, ralph in jersey is not easily deterred. I'm not one to let a little rubber roadblock get between me and smoking enjoyment. Armed with the thinnest of tapered round files and a seven-sixteenths aviation twist bit, in I bored. With the invaluable assistance of drugstore magnifying glasses and a powerful tensor lamp, I elongated that pin-prick of an airway, slowly but surely excavating an oval opening in my Peterson mouthpiece capable of actually passing tobacco smoke.

I know. A sharp tool in the hands of a clumsy non-professional is a prescription for disaster. But somehow, this time disaster was averted. The patron saint of pipe smokers, whoever he or she is, must have been sitting on my lap. Because against all odds, my birthday Peterson pipe survived its operation. Both the pipe and its original stem remain blissfully mated. In accordance with the higher laws governing estate pipes and Catholic marriages, like an old married couple they can now be expected to live out their remaining days together. But now, thanks to my risky surgery, they'll do it smoking like new. No, I'm being too modest. Now, for what portion of eternity the patron saint of smoking pipes allots to them, they will, together, smoke better than new!

Homogeneous Pack
Of Snarling Seamen

I find it strange how willing most everyone is to believe that the rules they've chosen to live by automatically apply to everyone else? It's the old "if it goes for the goose, then by golly it must go for the gander" train of thought, and it epitomizes a phenomenon I think of as "mental public transportation."

To grasp this concept fully, you must begin by envisioning the brain in your head as a car in a garage. Now, consider all the exotic places you can go in that little thinking jalopy you've got parked so conveniently just beneath the hair on your head. And remember, we've all got one! So why, as a sentient species, are we not a pack of freewheeling thought tourists, careening all over the intellectual globe in search of exotic ideas?

Sadly, it's because when it comes to matters of the brain, once some intrepid iconoclast grades a cerebral highway or lays down some track, humans will literally wear ruts across the surface of their wrinkly grey matter tracing and then retracing that exact same path. That's because humans are not explorers. Most of us are filthy stay-at-homes. At best we're commuters, dull-eyed, sleepy-headed strap-hangers on, yes, you guessed it, "mental public transportation."

Need convincing? Ask most anyone. Without so much as stopping to think, they'll blurt out, "Well, we're all damn sure in the same boat." True, when pressed there might be some divergence of opinion as to just what our boat looks like and where exactly it might be taking us, but the fact that we're all in it together, one big homogeneous pack of snarling seamen off on a grand shared voyage, this much is accepted social gospel.

I mention this because just about a year ago I sold a pipe I dearly loved. I did so because the pipe in question was a total jinx. It was the pipe I was smoking at work the day my filthy pig of a boss fired me for "sleeping at my desk." Sleeping my ass! Okay, yes, maybe my eyes were closed. But I was not sleeping. And even if I was, I don't snore so where's his proof? Two months later, as unlikely as it seems, it was this same pipe that tumbled sparking and smoldering onto my lap while I was zigzagging my car at an alarming rate of speed through infuriatingly slow rush hour traffic. The ensuing collision cost me the pain and suffering of a broken collar bone and four bruised ribs, as well as the nightmarish necessity of having to deal with the shuffling and grunting mud-people who inhabit my local body shop.

Now ralph in jersey is not a shaman or a Hopi medicine man or even a phony baloney gypsy fortune teller on the Atlantic City boardwalk. But self-preservation has required him, over the course of a calamitous lifetime, to learn to read simple handwriting on walls. And what those wall words were saying to me about my hexed up pipe was it was time for it to go. So I sent it off into the eBay ether, out where it would be scoffed up at a very reasonable price by an unsuspecting stranger.

It didn't seem like a particularly unethical thing to do at the time. Because, you see, ralph in jersey does not subscribe to the myth of shared human reality. He's the odd man out when it comes to that idea. That's because he's been forced to live out his existence on this planet according to a personal set of rules too bizarre for others to comprehend, much less share. He wouldn't wish his general condition on his worst enemy.

So when he sends off a cursed object in the U.S. mail from time-to-time, he fully expects that curse, a curse which is his alone, to end at the mail slot.

It's the same nifty disappearing act employed by Captain James T. Kirk to rid himself of all those pesky aliens that were forever trying to hitchhike a ride to Earth on his starship. First off, the troublesome space pests had to be rounded up and tricked into allowing themselves to be herded into a sealable escape pod. Once quarantined, the three-eyed non-humans could easily be fired off with the whoosh of a launch button into the imprisoning vastness of deepest, darkest space. That little "now you see them, now you don't" sleight of hand worked episode after episode for Captain James T. Kirk, and with the help of his auctioneer buddies at eBay, it's always worked for ralph in jersey in his dealings with voodoo pipes. That is, until now!

Because, you see, my accursed pipe has returned. Yesterday the Old Battleaxe came traipsing in the squeaking back door of our log cabin, the always present brown cigarette dangling from her brightly painted-up ruby lips, a small box in her hand. That little stamped-up cardboard sarcophagus was of a particular shape and size immediately recognizable to any hoarder of smoking pipes. No doubt about it. A new addition to my pipe family had arrived. It should have been no big deal. After all, pipe arrivals at ralph in jersey's cabin-in-the-woods home are about as frequent and regular as jet landings at Kennedy International Airport.

But the strange thing was, this time I had no recollection of having made any recent purchases. So, with all the piss-in-your-pants nervousness of a guy who's about to be told by a pregnant woman he has no memory of making love to that he's gonna be the father of her baby, I slowly peeled away the scotch tape bonds securing my ominous mystery bundle. Honestly, I had no idea what I was about to find.

And voila, what to my wondering eyes should appear was not a miniature sleigh and eight tiny reindeer, but rather my jinxed pipe. And it wasn't what was in that little box that shook me to my core, it was what wasn't. In that jumble of rubber-banded up pipe and bubble wrap and crumpled newspaper there was no note of explanation, no request for a refund. Simply a desperately unwanted pipe and its apparently fully-transferable curse returned to its merciless seller.

The pipe I can deal with. Pipes come. Pipes go. As a hoarder of pipes these are the bothersome triflings of my daily existence. But what was I to make of what was not here? Where were the written laments of the penny-pinching on-line purchasers, the unreasonable demands for financial reimbursement one comes to expect as a consequence of near every pipe transaction? In short, what was missing were all the reassuring signs and symbols that this was just one more inconsequential eBay transaction in a lifetime of inconsequential eBay transactions. All the physical signs pointed in one troubling direction. Was it conceivable that for once the United States Postal Service had failed ralph in jersey in its indispensible role as faithful expunger of personal curses? Just this once, it seemed the gander might actually have gotten what was no good for the goose. And if all this was true, what did the apparent contagion of this little pipe's jinx say about my long-held views on the non-transferability of pipe hexes and my cherished belief in separate human realities?

It seems like a billion years since I last strode the echoing halls of my high school. But I still recall a stick-thin geometry teacher with a silly, David Nivenesque mustache and a red English sports car lecturing us about how a theorem had to be considered invalid if it failed to satisfy an equation even a single time. No second chances for theorems. No grace period. No clemency. No consideration paid to any of the times it may have held up as a useful proof in the past. Fail once and you're through, kaput, out the door.

With a little reasonable extrapolation, the implications of that harsh love geometry lesson seem unmistakable when applied to my lone pipe in its note-less cardboard box. The voodoo or virus that governs the behavior of hexed up pipes seems to have mutated. It would appear to have commandeered for itself the ability to jump from one owner to the next. Something that was never true now seems undeniably so. Matters of conviction that for so long have felt rock-solid suddenly feel as flimsy as a house of cards. So needless to say, with the arrival of this most ominous package, some serious philosophical reevaluation is underway here in the cabin-in-the-woods home of ralph in jersey.

Trouble With Kippers

As anyone who's had the mixed pleasure of joining me for dinner at my woodsy cabin will attest, it is my habit to retire into the living room after a meal to enjoy a pipe. No forced march out into a Siberian garage or solemn tromp down dank basement steps for ralph in jersey. When I smoke in my own home, wife or no wife, I smoke where I please.

Does this mean I'm the king of my own castle? Not on your life! Like most married men, I abdicated my throne years ago in exchange for a little domestic peace and tranquility. But in this one thing, the smoking of my pipes when and where I please, some small vestige of ancient majesty abides.

It's a languid ritual for which I am well prepared. My smoking "setup" consists of a Decatur rack stocked with three or four preselected smoking pipes, two trusty tools, one a sterling silver tamper with a mustachioed cowboy's head for a knob and the other an el cheapo Czechoslovakian pick and spoon job, a tin of crispy tobak, a box of Blue Diamond kitchen matches and a fez-topped monkey man-servant whose one and only job is cradling my fuzzy cleaners in his chipped little porcelain monkey arms. Everything is kept on a small table just to the side of my "throne," which in actuality is nothing more than a busted down old Morris chair. Theoretically, once I get settled into that baby, everything I might need to enjoy my evening smoke should be an easy arm's reach away.

Kippers is the Old Battleaxe's scruffy orange tabby cat. Whenever I plunk myself down into that less than regal recliner, Kippers will invariably, with a single effortless bound hop up onto one of its wide oaken arms. What a stupid cat might hope to gain by executing such gymnastic shenanigans is beyond me. But cats being cats and having the reputation cats have, I suspect it's got something to do with curiosity.

In order to oblige this presumed interest in my pipe smoking, I've taken to exhaling heavy grey clouds of tobacco smoke directly into Kippers' whiskery puss.

And far from being put off by what I'd initially assumed would be his unpleasant initiation into the choking art of tobacco inhalation, Kippers seemed to take a positive liking to it. And even those words, "positive liking," don't do justice to the unbridled cat enthusiasm Kippers exhibited upon having his entire furry head engulfed in a virtual London fog of the very densest English pipe smoke. That old puss-puss positively licked his whiskers and purred with delight each and every time I sent a spicy plume wafting his way.

So this became our evening ritual. I'd plunk myself down deep into my tattered smoking chair and poor, addicted old Kippers would spring onto one of its broad arms. In would go the crispy tobacco shards — ralph in jersey takes his 'baccie dry, dry, dry — a match would be struck, and there we'd sit, man and furry pet, enjoying our smoke together almost as if we were brothers from different species mothers. Close as that!

It takes a big man to confess to such a foolish thing, but I was positively elated to have that cat's company. And perfect company Kippers was. Attentive in the extreme, his darting eyes switching back and forth between my busy hands and the pipe he'd come to crave, visibly mesmerized in that unique way cats get when their curiosity meters are banging on the rev limiter.

And yet, blessedly, because Kippers lacked even the most rudimentary capacity for human speech, there never once arose between us the need to make annoying small talk, the inane chitchat that passes for polite conversation but in actuality so often mars attempts at human smoking interaction.

It might have gone on like that to this very day if, stupid man that I am, I hadn't begun experimenting with different tobaccos. It must have been around Christmas that I made the tragic mistake of contacting the Canadian tobacco guru, Max Engel. I recklessly mailed him an astoundingly large check for the pleasure of sampling a very small silvery pouch-worth of his most excellent Compton's Macedonian Mixture. And Kawabunga! From the very first amazing puff I knew I'd at last found a blend worthy of comparison with my long gone and much lamented Balkan Sobranie White.

Kippers, being a cat of course, didn't know Balkan Sobranie from Bisquick Pancake Mix. But give that puss-puss his due. Man, that old tabby knew the good stuff the moment it hit his dry little nose. He let out a yowl of purest contentment, a sound eerily reminiscent of the otherworldly emanation Robert Mitchum lets out in NIGHT OF THE HUNTER when Lillian Gish tags him in the backside with a scatter gun. "Yeowwwwwwww!" And from that moment on, I swear, Kippers was a different animal.

Now I'm not saying there's anything wrong with having a favorite tobacco. God knows, I've got mine, and I'm not one to deny the lesser creatures theirs. But I do believe that crazy tabby took his predilection for one particular blend over all others to an unhealthy extreme. "Moderation in all things" is one of several nonsensical proverbs I've taken to heart for no good reason I can fathom. I preach them to anyone foolish enough to listen. But as it turned out, Kippers was not a moderate fellow. In fact, he proved himself to be one close-minded puss-puss. It seemed that in the matter of tobacco preferences I'd made the mistake of taking him to gay Paree, and now, hell or high water, there was to be no keeping him down on the farm. He could not be reasoned with. The high-handed little chap made it quite clear that it was his way or the highway, simple as that.

But I simply was not financially equipped to keep us both provisioned indefinitely with expensive Canadian weed, and Kippers took it hard. Refused to even sniff at our up-to-then perfectly acceptable go-to-blend, Butera's Royal Vintage Latakia #2. I'd blow a cloud of it up his snooter, and quick as that he'd hop down and meow to be let out the door. It hurt me to see him feeling so down.

So I went on-line and got us a premium sampler pack that included Dunhill's Mixture 95, Bell's Three Nuns, Squadron Leader and, go figure, a real zebra at the Derby, Erinmore Flake. But Kippers would have none of any of it. Begged to be let out and never came back.

The Old Battleaxe stapled signs with pictures of the stupid animal on poles around our neighborhood. Half out of her mind on vodka martinis, the shrew from Hell careened around our darkened streets with her head thrust out the window of her clapped-out Dodge Dart, shouting Kippers' name to god knows who as sparks from a half-smoked cigarette crackled upward into her bleached hair. What a show it was! But for two weeks she heard not so much as a meow in response to her desperate entreaties. Heartsick, exhausted and scorched to the roots, eventually the wife gave Kippers up for dead.

Then Ronnie Belks, a biker buddy of mine, told me he'd spotted a cat that looked a lot like Kippers stalking the tall brush behind the Belcher's Creek Towne Center, a little shopping spot located maybe a quarter mile down lake from our cabin. I took a ride to investigate. Kicked some grass and, at the risk of appearing as foolish as the wife, even called out for a bit. Then I went store to store, asking if anyone had seen an orange tabby that looked like he might be missing a meal or two.

My search ended in, of all places, the Village Smoke Shop. Kenny Burdette, the proprietor, is a long-time acquaintance of mine. Before I could even say hello, I spotted old Kippers curled up snoozing on the rug just behind one of the big comfy armchairs Kenny provides for his regulars. And far from looking destitute, the impression I had staring down at the old puss-puss was that he'd never looked fatter or more content.

Kenny confirmed my suspicions. The way he tells it, after a few days of watching the obviously homeless cat moping around his door, he'd bought a little plastic dish with fish pictures on it and a few cans of wet cat food. He'd put 'em on the floor of his shop, just inside the door, hoping to entice the hungry stray out of the cold. No such luck. But Saturday morning early, regular as clockwork, five stogie guys come strolling in for morning coffee and a communal puff. In no time at all, the cigar smoke in the shop gets so thick it flat-out overruns the commercial air purifier in the ceiling. So Kenny props a little plaster cigar store Indian in front of the door to hold it open, the idea being to let some fresh air in and some cigar fog out.

And who comes marching straight through that open door but Kippers. Hopped right up on the arm of the first recliner he came to, just like he was a lord high admiral stepping onto the bridge of his flagship. He put his little nose up and unmistakably began inhaling the peppery grey exhaust from five Dominican heaters. Damndest thing Kenny says he'd ever seen. In no time at all, the smoke-inhaling cat had the five stogie chewers in stitches. He was all they could talk about. And that night when Kenny went to lock up, Kippers inexplicably demanded to be locked up inside the shop.

He'd been there ever since, going on two weeks now. Every day when Kenny'd open up, their routine was the same. The cat, whom Kenny renamed Lord Alfred after the original patriarch of the famous London Dunhills, would graciously accept the bowl of food put down for him. Then he'd spring up onto the glass counter. Stationed directly in front of Kenny, in so many unspoken cat words he'd command the bemused proprietor to fire up his morning pipe. "The more smoke I blew straight into his kisser the better he liked it," Kenny noted in wonder. "And from then on, whenever a customer comes in and fires up, cigar or pipe, it makes no difference to that crazy cat, he'll literally leap up on him to get at the smoke."

As I listened to the happy tobacconist, I debated whether to tell him Lord Alfred, aka Kippers, was in point of fact my wife's pet. I weighed all the facts as I knew them to be. Yes, selfishly I wanted Kippers back. My evening smokes hadn't been the same since he left. But the look of crushing disappointment that had been etched all over his face the traumatic evening he first realized I was not going to continue supplying him with his precious Macedonian Mixture, that image haunted me. Could I, would I pony up a king's ransom in Canadian tobacco cash in order to purchase back the smoking companionship of my disloyal pet? I thought not.

So I stayed just long enough to share a bowl with Kenny and congratulate him on his rare good fortune. After all, how many small-town tobacco shops can boast of featuring a smoking cat? Kenny said he figured it was the smoke shop equivalent of a rinky-dink one-ring circus having a Bengal tiger or a two-headed man, and we both howled with laughter.

Then I left Lord Alfred right where he was, sleeping obliviously, content in the knowledge that in this, his new, self-invented role as a tobacco shop cat, he'd get all the tobacco smoke any feline could possibly want and more. And alas, if a nasty labor dispute should perhaps arise between cat and tobacconist sometime down the road, Lord Alfred demanding only the best and most expensive tobacco blends and cigar labels before performing his little trick, I figured it was better that Kenny should handle those negotiations rather than me.

So that's the way I left it. Just got in the car and came on home. Sure, yes, my half-stewed lush of a wife did ask if I'd seen her stupid cat. Bucked up by that surge of imperiousness a man gets whenever he's about to lie right to his wife's face, I put an end to the entire matter with an emphatic "No." Said it just as though it were a royal decree. Then I strolled into my living room lordly as you please, plunked down in my Morris chair and packed myself a bowl of Butera's Latakia #2.

About The Author

Ralph William Larsen was born in Brooklyn, New York. His spirit resides in Berkeley, California, although his body still remains trapped in a mountainous region of northern New Jersey. He continues to refer to his writing as being "inside out." By this verbal contrivance he hopes to convey to his reader some inkling of what it is that keeps him writing at all. Because while fellow clatterers seem intent on bearing down on the big picture, beheading sentences and pillaging whole paragraphs in their "take no prisoners" campaigns to get finished stories between covers, this author accepts it as his lot to be habitually caught up in the nuts and bolts. It's not that he disdains the story. It's just that he loves the sentence to distraction. It's always been so. Consider this. When afforded the honor of addressing his hero, Norman Mailer, all he could think to say was, "I don't believe you ever quite got around to writing the Great American Novel, but in my opinion you wrote the Great American Sentence many times over." And he meant it as a high compliment, no matter how badly the remark was taken by the older author. Because for ralph in jersey, always, the be-all and end-all of time spent before a keyboard is the sentence. He begins his tales with no clear idea of how they will develop. Endings are nowhere in sight. Undeterred, he commences each new verbal contrivance in the hope that if he stays with it long enough, straddles it in his mind like Old Ahab on the back of his white whale, stabbing, always stabbing away at its heart, then perhaps smaller things will come. So like his spiritual brother-in-arms the deep-sea fisherman, ralph in jersey lashes himself to his swivel chair, hook baited, hoping against hope with the casting of each new line that a great fish of a sentence will rise.

31799460R00158

Made in the USA
Lexington, KY
24 February 2019